Salvation is impossible.

Independently published.

All places, people and organisations are completely made up for the purposes of this novel. Any similar people, places or organisations are completely unintended and a coincidence.

This story contains scenes you may find distressing. There is rape and child abuse in it as well as violence and bad language. Readers are advised to contact the following organisations.

Childline. 0800 1111

UNICEF. www.UNICEF.org

www.gov.uk

www.womansaid.org.uk

Child abuse: useful organisations

This advice applies to Scotland. Where the novel is set. Some of it might be useful if you live elsewhere in the UK.

Organisations for children and young people

ChildLine (Scotland)
NSPCC Scotland
Templeton House
62 Templeton Street
Glasgow
G40 1DA
Tel: 0141 420 3816
ChildLine: 0800 1111
Email: scotland@nspcc.org.uk
Website: www.nspcc.org.uk

Children 1st
83 Whitehouse Loan
Edinburgh
EH9 1AT
Tel: 0131 446 2300
Email: cfs@children1st.org.uk
Children 1st Parentline: 08000 28 22 33
Email: parentlinescotland@children1st.org.uk
Website: www.children1st.org.uk

Scottish Child Law Centre
91 George Street
Edinburgh
EH2 3ES
Adviceline: 0131 667 6333, Monday to Friday 9.30am to 4.00pm
Freephone for under 21s: 0800 328 8970 (landlines) or 0300 330 1421 (mobiles)
Administration: 0131 668 4400
Email: enquiries@sclc.org.uk
Legal advice email: advice@sclc.org.uk
Website: www.sclc.org.uk

Clan Childlaw Edinburgh
Norton Park
57 Albion Road
Edinburgh
EH7 5QY
Tel: 0808 129 0522 (freephone)
Text: 07527 566682 (texts will be charged at the normal network rate)
Email: info@clanchildlaw.org
Website: contact form
Website: www.clanchildlaw.org

Clan Childlaw Glasgow
Wellpark Enterprise Centre
120 Sydney Street
Glasgow
G31 1JF
Tel: 0808 129 0522 (freephone)

Text: 07527 566682 (texts will be charged at the normal network rate)
Email: info@clanchildlaw.org
Website: contact form
Website: www.clanchildlaw.org

Organisations for parents.

ParentLine Scotland

Helpline: 0800 028 2233 (Mon-Fri 9.00am-9.00pm)
Email: parentlinescotland@children1st.org.uk
Website: www.children1st.org.uk

General organisations

Rape Crisis Scotland

3rd Floor
Abbey House
10 Bothwell Street
Glasgow
G2 6LU
Tel (General Enquiries): 0141 331 4180 (Monday to Friday 9am to 4pm)
Free Helpline: 08088 01 03 02 (every day 6pm to midnight)
Minicom: 0141 353 3091
For support by email: support@rapecrisisscotland.org.uk

General
email: info@rapecrisisscotland.org.uk
Website: www.rapecrisisscotland.org.uk

National Society for the Prevention of Cruelty to Children (NSPCC)
42 Curtain Road
London
EC2A 3NH
Helpline: 0808 800 5000
Textphone: 18001 0808 800 5000
Text messages: 88858
Email: help@nspcc.org.uk or online form to report concerns about a child
Website: www.nspcc.org.uk

Csethesigns.scot

The Scottish government set up the csethesigns.scot website to tackle child sexual exploitation. It provides information and advice for young people and for parents about how to spot the warning signs and symptoms, common myths and practical advice for staying safe online and offline.

Organisations for adults who experienced childhood abuse

A range of organisations can support survivors of abuse living in Scotland.

Future Pathways
Survivor Telephone: 0808 164 2005
(Monday to Friday 10.00am to 6.00pm)
Email: registration@futurepathways.co.uk
Website: www.future-pathways.co.uk

National Association for People Abused in Childhood (NAPAC)
Support line: 0808 801 0331
Monday to Thursday 10am to 9pm, Friday 10am to 6pm
Calls are free from landlines and mobiles. They will not show on a phone bill.
Email: online contact form
Website: napac.org.uk

Speak Out Scotland (S.O.S.)
Suite 1/2
15 North Claremont Street
Glasgow
G3 7NR
Tel: 0141 332 9326
Email: info@speakoutscotland.org

Website: www.speakoutscotland.org

Stop It Now! UK & Ireland

Stop It Now! Scotland offers a wide range of services to the public and professionals aimed both at the prevention of child sexual abuse and support for those affected. Their Scotland office can be contacted on 0131 556 3535 during office hours and by email at scotland@stopitnow.org.uk.

Stop It Now! UK & Ireland
Helpline: 0808 100 0900 (freephone)
Helpline email: help@stopitnow.org.uk
Website: www.stopitnow.org.uk

SurvivorsUK

SurvivorsUK provide information, support and counselling for male victims/survivors of rape and sexual abuse, as well as their family and friends.

SurvivorsUK
11 Sovereign Close
London
E1W 3HW

Text-based helpline: 020 3322 1860
(Monday to Friday from 10.30am to 9pm;
Saturday and Sunday 10am to 6pm)
WhatsApp-based helpline: 07491 816064
Office tel: 020 3598 3898 (Monday to Friday
from 9.30am to 5pm)
Email: info@survivorsuk.org
Website: www.survivorsuk.org

Trauma Counselling Line Scotland

Trauma Counselling Line Scotland (TCLS) provides confidential telephone counselling to any adult who was abused in childhood. The contact details are:

Trauma Counselling Line Scotland
Tel: 08088 020 406 (freephone) (Monday to Wednesday 2.00pm to 6.00pm, Friday 9.00am to 3.00pm). You can leave a message at all other times.
Email: contactus@health-in-mind.org.uk
Website: www.health-in-mind.org.uk

Victim Support Scotland

Victim Support Scotland provides support and information services to victims and witnesses of crime in Scotland.

Victim Support Scotland
15/23 Hardwell Close
Edinburgh
EH8 9RX
Tel: 0131 668 4486
Scottish Helpline: 0800 160 1985 (Monday to Friday 8am to 8pm)
UK Supportline: 0808 168 9111 (Weeknights 8pm to 8am; Weekends Saturday 5pm to Monday 8am)
Email: info@victimsupportsco.org.uk
Website: victimsupport.scot

Wellbeing Scotland

Wellbeing Scotland is a voluntary organisation with services across Scotland, providing a range of holistic services for individuals (both children and adults) and families whose life experiences have impacted negatively on their wellbeing. These include therapeutic services specialising in abuse and trauma work.

Wellbeing Scotland
14 Bank Street
Alloa
FK10 1HP

Helpline: 0800 121 6027 (Monday to Friday 9.00am to 11.00am)
Office tel: 01324 630 100
Email: info@wellbeingscotland.org
Website: contact form
Website: www.wellbeingscotland.org

I hope this is useful for you.

Dedicated to the real Blueberry Muffin who in real life I made out of tights. She is a cute doll.

Special thanks.

For the pacing nervous man in the bus station and the lady sitting near stance eight with the kid in black. You inspired this story.

Also to Chris. My proof-reader.

Chapters.

Chapter One

Tenth of November two thousand and twenty three.

She sat there with her blue jeans on black shoes and green, red fleece filled hooded jacket on. Her bleached dark brown hair and pointy nose made her look like a drug user that was coming down from a high.

Her faded blue jeans had seen better days and she travelled with a young smallish dark haired boy dressed in black.

That boy was her son. He was called John Watt. He was the oldest.

John had three brothers and two sisters. The twin brothers were called Richard and Dominic and his other brother was called Stephen junior. His two sisters were twins as well. They were called Agatha and Chrissy. John looked after them all and they were worried about their mum. She drank alcohol like a fish breathes water. By which I mean she was a raging alcoholic who hated people and a mean cow when drunk.

Her name was Alice Pidgeon, and she was wanted for an attack on a helpless disabled girl who had autism. The attack had left the girl badly shaken but unhurt.

How had Alice's life come to this? Wanted by the police for a terrible thing. She didn't know.

Thirty eight years ago. Tenth of November nineteen eighty five.

"One last push."

The woman pushed hard. A baby girl appeared crying loudly. The baby girl was named Alice Pidgeon after her grandmother. Her grandmother was honoured by the news.

There was no father on the birth certificate. Her mother was unmarried and afraid.

The grandparents begged. "Let us raise young Alice Pidgeon and you can move on with your life."

The mother agreed. Alice Pidgeon would be raised by her grandmother and grandfather. The mother was paid ten thousand pounds to move on with her life and forget Alice.

The baby Alice Pidgeon cried a lot. Her grandmother tried to soothe her. She dipped the baby's dummy tit into a pot of honey and gave it to Alice.

Alice liked it. She also liked being held and cuddled. Pity she didn't get much of that. She got fed and winded. Just not cuddled.

Two years later. The year is nineteen eighty seven.

Alice missed her mum. She had been told that her grandmother was her mother. The sad thing was that her grandmother was not able to show affection to her. Alice knew that she wasn't her real mother. Finding the birth certificate at two year old proved it.

“You are not my mother.”

“I'm the best you have.”

“My real mother would hug me.”

“Your mother is dead.” The grandmother lied.

Alice Pidgeon burst into tears and ran into her room.

The grandparents locked her in.

They let her out at dinner time. She was too young to be left alone.

Thirty years ago.

Tenth of November nineteen ninety one.

At eight years old on the tenth of November. Alice was taught how to cook. Alice having forgotten about the last time asked. “Who is my mother?”

The grandparents were taken aback. Alice Pidgeon must never find out the truth.

“She's dead love. Now go and cook the dinner.”

Alice Pidgeon screaming like a banshee ran into her room and cried bitterly.

The grandmother locked the door.

Only at four o'clock and getting close to dinner time when Alice knocked on the door demanding to be let out did the horrible evil grandmother unlock the door. And young Alice had to cook the dinner still. It was always Alice's job to cook the dinner now.

Today’s dinner was a roast chicken dinner. Today was Sunday.

Alice was so upset that she done a terrible job at cooking the dinner. She burnt the potatoes and carrots and spoiled the gravy.

The chicken was frazzled and black. It looked like someone had taken a electric power supply unit and plugged it into the chicken.

Also the chicken was still raw in places. Alice was told by her grandmother. “There's no dinner for you.” Before being forcibly sent to her room with no dinner.

The grandparents ate up the burnt dinner. They soon regret it.

Disease strikes them.

The grandparents lie in bed moaning and groaning. Eight year old Alice Pidgeon was rushed off her feet looking after them. Alice is soon exhausted by the running about.

Her grandparents get sicker and weaker. Soon they reach a critical condition.

Alice finally calls the doctors in. The doctors call social services. Alice is taken to a children's home as her grandfather goes into cardiac arrest.

Alice gets a message from the hospital. Her grandparents are dying. Alice tried to tell the workers that her grandfather and grandmother need her, but nobody listens to the eight year old Alice. Alice sobs bitterly waiting for the phone call.

Alice is soon taken to the hospital and the doctors ignore her. They have other patients to see. Finally, one of the junior doctors talks to her.

“I'm so sorry. Your grandfather passed away just after the phone call we sent you. He went into cardiac arrest and couldn't be saved. Your grandmother is dying. Doctors can't treat her anymore. She's in here.” The junior doctor Matilda Brown pulls back a curtain and a uncomfortable looking grandmother appears into view.

“Grandmother.” Alice Pidgeon screams with delight. She is so happy to see her grandmother again.

The grandmother takes off her oxygen mask weakly. “I need to tell you something. It's important. Your real mother is my daughter, and she is still alive. I sent her away. Unmarried mother. I don't know who your father is. Find your mother. Find your father. Live your life.”

The heart-rate dips down and the nurses put the oxygen mask back on the older Alice Pidgeon.

The grandmother fights them but is too weak to fight.

Alice sobs bitterly and hugs her grandmother. “I love you Gran.” she says gently as her grandmother starts to sigh deeply. As Alice kisses her grandmother on the forehead, alarms start ringing.

The eight year old Alice Pidgeon is forced to watch as doctors try to bring back the seventy eight year old Alice Pidgeon back from the dead. She screams with frustration at her new carers. Then screams even more at the doctors for failing to bring back her grandmother and grandfather.

Two weeks later. Twenty forth of November nineteen ninety one.

Wrapped up in a scarf and winter clothes Alice sobs bitterly as her grandmother's coffin goes into the ground on top of her grandfather's coffin in the cold freezing ground.

The other mourners shiver in the minus five cold air. They stomp about trying so very hard to keep warm and failing miserably.

It is worse for the priest. He can barely turn the pages of the bible.

The priest feels his fingers going numb. He feels them turning blue. He uttered the sacred prayers and called for the community to give support to young Alice.

Alice was too upset to communicate her wish to go home. If they understood that, they would have taken her home. Either they didn’t understand or didn’t care.

Alice Pidgeon was not going anywhere. Not until the service was over.

A plate was passed around. The eight people gathered put fifty pence each on the tin plate. Alice put in a pound coin with the queen’s head on it.

When the plate had been passed around the small bit of money was given to Alice.

Alice took it all. The money was her money. She had five pounds to her name. She hoped that the life insurance policy for both her grandparents would pay out. Or it was going to cost Alice and Social Work a fortune.

If the life insurance policies paid out, Alice could continue to live in her grandmother's house with support from the government and a carer. Alice hoped it would pay out.

The drive to the life insurance policy place at Lifeisus was terrifying. Alice Pidgeon knew that if the money didn't get paid out, she would end up in a children's home. And not a nice children's home. A creepy one with spiders and watching eyes.

Alice prayed that the money would pay out. It had to.

The bright purple heart rate monitor logo showed a neon orange heart beat with the yellowy pink words Lifeisus.

Alice looked terrified of the mascot standing there. A huge neon orange heart that looked scary with its huge neon green teeth and red gummy smile. It looked like a monster.

It was called a life insurance monster. And it was poorly stitched together. You could see the seams showing through the paint and it looked like something a child with no sewing skills could put together in five minutes. It was ugly. Very ugly. Obviously cheaply made.

When they got to the bright purple and orange themed hideous office with hideous cave like paintings on the wall that a two year old could have done and probably did do. Alice walked over to the expensive oak desk and took a seat at the customer side of the expensive looking desk while the social worker waited outside in the foyer.

A man entered the room and sat at the desk on the other side to Alice. It took five minutes of silence for him to determine Alice's fate.

"We are not paying out."

"Why not?"

"Act of God. Your grandmother and grandfather died because of god's will. Act of God. Case dismissed."

"I need the money. You have to pay out." The eight year old Alice begged the man sitting at the other end of a very expensive desk.

"Nope sorry. Still not paying out." The man said grinning at the thought of the money he had saved by not paying out money from the life insurance policies and conning the poor elderly people that opened life insurance policies in the first place.

"If only they still had workhouses." The man thought to himself as Alice Pidgeon roared her frustrated feelings for the first time.

"You sir are nothing more then a conman conning the old folk into paying out money for life insurance policies and never paying out." Alice Pidgeon roared loudly.

"We pay out for murder. That's all we pay out for."

"So, if my grandfather and grandmother were murdered you would pay out."

"Only if it wasn't you who killed them, or you had nothing to do with it."

"They were murdered. By a monster."

"Sweetie. They both died of food poisoning caused by a undercooked chicken. Not murdered. Just God's will."

Alice bursts into tears and storms out the room. With no money coming in now, she must now sell her grandmother's house to pay the costs of the funeral and her care costs. She will be placed in a children's home and cared for.

The children's home is full of children. These are sad children who have forgotten how to play and those few that remember how to play have few toys to play with.

The building itself is dark and creepy. It's gloomy windows set the scene for a horror movie not suitable for children to watch. The creaky doors and gate need badly oiled, and the windows haven't been opened for years.

Its called Pleasure Zone. A children's home called Pleasure Zone suggests a fun happy place. It's not a happy place at all.

Legend has it this was a hospital once. A place where people came to die.

Alice Pidgeon takes a deep breath and opens the door. The hallway looks like something from the Adams family. Maybe they lived here. Alice looks around expecting to see a hand appear on the stairs.

"See Alice. The children's home isn't that bad." A social worker lies.

They have put her in the cheapest option available. They must save money somehow. Alice eats like a horse.

At dinner time Alice has second helpings of fish and chips and apple pie and ice cream. She is nicknamed greedy by the workers and sent to her room after dinner.

Alice could have done with a third helping of both parts of the meal. The kids portion seemed too small for one kid. Maybe a four year old could be filled up but a eight year old wouldn't be. It was worse for the teens. They were given the small portion too. If they complained about the size of the meal they were sent to bed with no dinner.

It was a very strict children's home. Alice felt very unhappy here.

As time went on Alice lost her baby fat and became gaunt looking. Her eyes became sad and she felt alone. But she didn't know she was about to make a friend in the most excellent way.

She bumped into them. Literally. It was Halloween in nineteen ninety two. Alice was dressed in a werewolf costume. The other girl wore a black dress with a black cape.

"Oh, sorry I didn't know you were there."

"It's ok. Dressed in black isn't my usual style. Prefer pink dresses."

"What's your name?"

"Tuesday."

"Are you related to Wednesday?"

"Nope. Mum named me Tuesday because I was born on a Tuesday. My mum has alcohol issues. That's why I'm here."

"You are a girl the same as me."

"Yip. I am a woman, and you are a girl. That's why I have my own bathroom and you must still share."

"How old are you?"

"Eleven years old. I just started last week."

"Started what."

"When you get a bit older the staff will tell you about periods and woman stuff. You are still too young to know this stuff."

"Can you please tell me now? I would like to be prepared."

Tuesday smiled and shook her head. "I would ask the staff." She answered sweetly before moving away from the stairs. Alice watched her in awe.

They met again at dinner time. Tuesday ran into the dining hall and sat down hoping nobody had noticed the black bag of sanitary pads beside her. She had only just finished her first period and was unsure when the next one was due.

Nobody said anything about the bag. They didn't know what it was. Alice knew nothing about periods. She knew woman were allowed to use handbags. She didn't know why?

A female staff member asked Tuesday if her periods were finished for the first time. Tuesday reported to her left ear that she had just finished her first period.

Alice heard the word periods and asked the staff member. "What are periods?"

The staff member grimaced. "I will tell you about periods when you are a bit older." She explained to Alice. "You are too young to understand the situation just now, maybe wait a couple of years before we have the talk."

Alice sighs deeply. "Ok." She said hoping that the staff would talk to her more.

Johnny Button who was a staff member grimaced at the awkward moment. “Come to my office at once Alice.”

Seventeen girls all called Alice and all with different surnames looked up.

“Alice Pidgeon. Come to my office please.” Johnny Button sighed.

Alice Pidgeon gulped. She put down her knife and fork on a half eaten dinner, stood up, and stepped away from the dining table. She followed the annoyed Johnny Button with great caution. She was worried about being in trouble.

She had every right to be worried.

Every right.

Johnny liked kids for one thing only. He liked the power he had over them. Alice didn’t know the danger she was in.

Chapter two

Tenth of November two thousand and twenty three. ten am.

As I sat waiting for Chris sitting on one of the seats in the bus station somewhere between the statue of the two lovers and the big fancy clock, I noticed a man looking odd.

The man at first glance looked like a father to be waiting for a birth. His striped grey and black polo shirt hidden under his black hoodie jacket make him look at odds in the bus station. They didn't match his dirty blue jeans. His short styled straight red hair was puffed up on his head and his red Hitler moustache was connected to his bushy red beard and made him look like a leprechaun. His blob nose and the fact his eyes darted from left to right as well as the fact that he was chewing gum furiously showed me that he was tense. Very tense. He had his hands in his pockets and was pacing the floor. I noticed as he paced that he had a white scar on the back of his head like a comma. His thick bushy eyebrows and his huge sticky out ears like king Charles made him look ugly. His jeans didn't match the black Nike air trainers he was wearing. The trainers had a white tick on them.

I wondered where I had seen him before. Maybe on a wanted poster.

I looked away as he glared at me. Someone came over to him. I didn't see who just a blur of yellow hair wearing a red dress but by the time I glanced his way again properly he was gone and the someone else was with him.

I hoped that he had a first date and was not the slasher that I had heard about.

The famous slasher was always wearing a mask. A single silly clown mask. He also wore an apron over his black coat and wore on his feet black Nike air trainers with a white tick.

Trainers just like those ones.

Surely not. He didn't look the type. Did he?

I had checked for blood on the trainers but I was too far away to see any visible blood.

It didn't mean that they were clean.

Also, blood doesn't show much on black. Try having a bloody nose at work once and you will see what I mean.

I breathed a sigh of relief as the man left and breathed another sigh of relief when my darling sweetheart Chris Morgan comes near me.

"Hi Chris." I purr to my darling sweetheart as he kisses me.

"Hi Elizabeth" He grins back. He sounds sexy.

I feel sexy.

Our date goes well and we have a wonderful time eating brunch in Glasgow.

I get back home in time to see the six-o clock news. The other someone comes on screen. She is blonde haired and blue eyed wearing a red dress and red shoes.

Her name is Janice Alice Martin. She is nineteen years old.

She was missing. It wasn't like her to go missing. Her parents put an appeal for information.

She was last seen at ten am.

The time I saw her leave with the man.

A number comes on screen and people are urged to call if they have information about the case.

I phone the number. "Police please."

A policewoman answers.

“Hello.” She sighs.

I start talking.

As I talk a builder works tiding up the building site in wild and windy weather. As he works, he feels a hand tap him on the shoulder. He looks behind him and sees a single silly clown mask.

He is terrified of clowns.

“Ha ha very funny, if you are five. Come out. Come out where ever you are.”

Nothing replies to his plea.

“It’s not funny man. I am bloody terrified and you know it.”

The scaffolding falls and he is taken from behind.

He struggles to break free. The black blob with the green eyes takes him before the scaffolding breaks down and the storm gets stronger.

The black blob grabs the clown mask and flees.

Before he leaves, he cuts a deep scar in the shape of a cross on his victim's left breast.

The slasher has stuck again.

I finish talking and hang up.

The bleeping starts on the builder's phone. His second job is calling.

The patient is crashing on the operating table.

The surgeon is nowhere in sight. The storm outside gets stronger. The trainee surgeon tries to save him.

The storm gets worse. The trainee surgeon starts CPR. The nurses' empty vials of blood as a young police officer watches in horror.

"He will be all right boss. Won't he?" She says tears falling from her eyes.

"He has to be." Her boss says grimly. "You are not allowed to die at work. Ricki said so. Also, you must be at work for twenty four hours a day if you are the police. Ricki says so."

The police officer nodded. She knew the prime minster Ricki Sinak had made this law only last week. She also remembered that she was lucky to be alive today after facing the robbery that had went wrong and the gun being fired. Her co worker had taken the bullet. The bullet that had been meant for her. Her co worker had been two days away from getting a nice cosy desk job instead of being out there finding the needle in the haystack that was the slasher.

The slasher. That was what the press had dubbed him. That is if he was a male. For all they knew he could be a woman. The victims were all different but had one thing in common. They all were women. All from the area of Glasgow and surrounding areas. Like Paisley and North Ayrshire to name but a few. Some gay. Some straight. Some black. Some white. Some of Asian descent. Some African.

One sixteen year old. The third youngest of the victims so far was twenty-three and a chemist. Blonde but smart enough to hand meds out without making mistakes.

You have to be very smart to hand meds out. Genius level smart. Not Garnock Academy level which is one level above stupid.

The police officer sobbed as the nurses covered the man. They had tried and failed to save him.

The storm died down.

The police were called out again. The police officer and her boss stayed at the hospital and stayed with the family as they were told the bad news. The police officer was then sent to catch the robbers that had killed her partner Martin Alan Peters.

The date changed from the tenth of November two thousand and twenty three to the eleventh of November two thousand and twenty three. It was 00.00.00 am. A second later it was 00.00.01. The police officer got in the car and sat there. She sobbed bitterly and furiously into the steering wheel.

“Why must you die Martin?” She sobbed. Honking the horn in anger while tears flooded her cheeks.

She didn’t know how long she had sat there. But the dawn starting to break disturbed her.

She became aware of the swallows and the sparrows as well as the crows, seagulls, doves and the quiet cooing of the pigeons. The tears still fell.

Then there was a tap on her window. She turned to her right, saw a pregnant woman wearing an oxygen mask on her face and a red dress and rolled down the window.

“Can I help you miss?” She asked before feeling blood dripping down her back. She turned around and saw a clown masked black clothed figure running away empty handed. “Help” She shouted before passing out. As she passed out, she noticed she was in a parking spot for nurses. She had seen it but as she was police, she had thought it was ok to park there. She hadn't locked the door of her car. She begged to live as the darkness took her.

Bleep. Bleep. The heart monitor bleeped loudly. The sound of air rushing into a mask was reassuring. The gentle breaths in and out meant one thing.

She was alive.

She remembered the Nike trainers. She remembered the clown mask. But not much else.

It wasn't surprising really. She had been dead for twenty minutes. They had nearly given up on her.

She didn't know that. Just knew she had been dreaming. Dreaming about God. Dreaming that she was dead. She had dreamt she was in heaven with her partner Martin.

She tried to move but couldn't. She seemed to be strapped down.

The needle went in. She fell into a deep dreamless sleep.

At zero seven hundred hours two minutes and nine seconds on the eleventh of November two thousand and twenty three Katie Elsa Young was put into an induced coma after being attacked in the hospital car park in the nurse's parking bay just before dawn.

Her workmates tried to find the attacker.

Eleventh of November two thousand and twenty three. Two thirty two am.

The attacker was waiting for the bus. Still in black clothes and wearing his mask. His standing dummy beside him.

Inside the bump was unused masking tape and a knife that he had bought that day from the local supermarket with the blue label beginning with t.

He had a body to deal with at base.

A dead blonde-haired woman in a red dress.

He planned to cut her up and dump her in a skip. There was one or two that he knew of dotted around the place. There was one in Hope Street as well as Bothwell Street. If he had to, he could find others.

First, he took the dress off. He found it fiddly and awkward and the dress got ripped as he removed it. Then he put the body in the bath before cutting the head off and the limbs off the torso.

Finally, he cut the torso in two or tried to. The spine got in the way of the knife, and it broke.

He swore under his breath. The f curse word. He swore repeatedly when he saw he had cut himself on the thumb with the knife.

His blood could catch him out he knew. He hadn't served time before now and he was dammed if he was serving time. He would rather die first.

He grabbed the red dress and covered his thumb with it hoping nobody heard him before running the tap to wash the body parts before bagging them up in thick black bags.

A few drops of blood got into the bags. He didn't notice it. He was too busy thinking of getting to the skip and back without being seen. He took his clown mask off. It was hot now. He needed a drink. He changed into a pink tracksuit and walked to the skip with the bags in tow.

Nobody saw anything odd. He was just some guy putting out the rubbish. His red hair worked with his pink tracksuit. It looked smart. Almost trendy.

He touched his bushy beard. He needed to shave. But tonight, he will drink with friends and tell them the lie that he was ditched by his latest girlfriend for a rich doctor.

It will get him the sympathy vote.

He will drink well tonight.

Eleventh of November two thousand and twenty three. Three am.

At the pub he got chatting to a young blonde-haired girl who was thirty five years old. She had blue eyes and was very fat.

Her name was Jennifer and she didn't work for the NHS. She was in training to be a school teacher and was very cruel to the kids she was in charge of. She hated the smart ones as they used to show her up.

She bullied them. She used to call them names. Useless was a term she used of them. If she was in a good mood of course.

If she was in a bad mood, she punished them harshly for tiny crimes by making them scrub the toilets with a toothbrush. Male, female and unisex ones. All cleaned by the same toothbrush.

Talking in class was just one of these tiny crimes. Bulling was allowed. If you were bullied by the other kids you were punished for standing out.

Then the teacher bullied you more. Not only that but the victim had to apologise to the bully for letting them bully him or her.

After the apology was given the victim was harassed even more and punished for being bullied. Needless to say, bulling was spreading in her school garnock academy like the black death in the Middle Ages. Just nobody owned up to being bullied that was all.

Not even the ones who were bullied constantly by everyone else admitted it. They were having to say sorry for being born.

Jennifer loved bulling them. They reminded her of an old victim of hers. Elizabeth Louisa Mullen. A young kid with Asperger's with a brother with autism. Her fiancée was normal apart from his left arm. Jennifer had loved calling her names and forcing her to eat cold chips off the floor at school.

Jennifer didn't know that Elizabeth was now a world-famous author who "people watched" in her spare time. That was how the press put it. The truth was Elizabeth noticed stuff more then other people. Maybe it was the Asperger's. Maybe it was a result of years of constant bulling. Elizabeth was great at spotting stuff. It was like she ran on instinct. Instinct that would have kept her ancestors alive in Africa millions of years ago.

Instinct that kept her alive and watching her back.

Jennifer never had to watch her back. She had lots of school friends and bullied helpless children mercilessly.

Jennifer swapped numbers with the man she had met. He also had been a bully at school. He wanted to meet up with her but wasn't sure if she was free.

She agreed to meet up with him in Glasgow on the twenty first of November two thousand and twenty three at half eleven on the dot.

Twenty first of November two thousand and twenty three. Ten am.

The bus station was busy. The body of the blonde woman in the red dress had been found that morning chopped up in the skip full of building materials.

Naturally the police were looking for a builder who knew the Glasgow area.

The young police officer saw the body and noticed a cross on her left breast on her chest.

She knew then that the slasher had struck again.

Chapter three

Halloween two thousand and six.

seventeen years ago.

The slasher hadn't started out evil. He had brain damage from a traumatic birth.

He had been stuck in the birth canal.

His mother had panicked. It seemed to be taking forever. Why wouldn't it move?

"Push." The yelling woman roared.

Chrissy Rice pushed as hard as she could but nothing happened.

“Push harder.” The yelling woman roared again.

Chrissy started thinking about that day. The day that had ruined her life and left her with a stuck baby inside her.

The bad man opening a unlocked door. The terrifying struggle in the night. The attack that stole her virginity. The police officers claiming that she was lying about the attack. That she wasn’t raped because nobody heard her scream.

The reason she didn’t scream. Fear. The loss of her voice in the attack. The struggle to breathe. The heart pounding terrible fear. Thinking she was going to die.

The police officers had to lie about the attack. He was one of their own. The worst thing was he had done it before. Other women. Same outcome. Not believed.

She pushed down harder pooing the bed in the process. Still no sign of baby.

The baby's heart rate dipped.

"We need you to really push this baby out." The midwife yelled.

Chrissy pushed again. Nothing gave way.

The baby's heart slowed down again. It reached a dangerous low level.

The midwife yelled and pulled the cord. "Emergency c section needed now." Chrissy's labour on Halloween night would soon be over.

Ten minutes later Chrissy was holding a baby boy in her arms. The baby boy was gasping his first breaths.

Chrissy looked horrified. He looked just like his father. "Take him. His name is Damien." She begged the midwife. "I was raped by his father."

"You are his mother. He needs you." The midwife whispered gently.

Meanwhile the baby fought for his life as his mother fought to give him up.

Alarms sounded in the operating theatre.

A cry of concern. “My baby.”

The doctors and nurses start work on Damien. He had breathed in the first poop and it was affecting his lungs.

Five minutes goes by. Then ten.

The baby doesn’t respond.

Twenty minutes goes by.

The baby stops breathing.

Another five minutes go by and the doctors decide there’s no hope.

Then a gasp comes from baby.

Damien is alive.

It is dubbed the Halloween miracle.

Ten years later.

A young red haired boy is on his own at a Halloween party. He tells the staff it’s his birthday. The staff laugh at him. The boy Damien grabs a sharp kitchen knife and hides in the toy cupboard. The staff play the yearly game of Halloween hide and seek with the other kids in the children's home.

One staff member goes into the cupboard and sees Damien has a knife. It is the last thing she sees as Damien viciously stabs her twenty times and leaves her dead in the cupboard.

By the time police are called. Damien is the only survivor of the Halloween massacre. All the other staff and children are dead at the scene.

The police arrest an innocent man on the word of the terrified Damien Rice. Damien's word and the planted evidence from Damien means that Jordan Woods is in time found guilty of forty five counts of murder. His young son Ryan Woods will grow up without a dad. Damien on the other hand will be treated as a hero.

Seven years later.

Seven years after the massacre a body is found in the local community centre garden at five o’clock in the morning by a red haired girl walking her dog.

The body is named as Ann Smith. She was smothered by a red scarf and a cross is carved into the left breast of the woman.

She is not the first victim to be found. Another one had been found in the garden as well. In fact two bodies in total had been found so far.

Ann was the second to be found. The first victim was a young thirteen year old woman called Susan D Banks who was covered in make up to make her look older. The thirteen year old woman had been found in the garden close to the body of the second victim. Both bodies had the cross carved into their left breast. They were smothered by the same red scarf.

The red scarf meanwhile is nowhere to be found.

The next day. November the first. Eleven am.

A young police officer called Ryan Woods is waiting for his boss on the first day of his new job.

His boss the older and smarter Elizabeth Jean Mackay walks slowly to her desk and with eyes watching like a hawk sees the young officer remain standing as he waits for his boss to speak.

The white room which is full of black furniture including the desk and standard black office chair looks like an art gallery dedicated to the grandkids of the older boss. It is full of colourful flowers and plants and unusual animals that look like something only a three year old, a two year old and a five year old can draw.

You would think that the boss had dedicated her office to the grandkids. You would also be right.

On the desk is a laptop. The laptop is plugged in and open. It is also switched on. A picture of three young grandkids fill the screen. A folder appears marked click me.

The boss clicks the folder.

Crime reports are opened. Two new ones need attention.

At last the boss speaks.

“I need you to check these crime reports and see if we have caught anyone yet. I am sending you the email now.”

The boss goes into her emails, types the email, adds the files then sends the email to the new officer.

Ryan sighs. He was hoping for some action.

Suddenly a panicking call comes from the radio. “Back up needed. Officer down. Officer Grace Addison is missing.”

The officer Mark Thompson shouts down the radio fighting the strong urge to sleep. He knew with his stab wound to the chest that if he fell asleep he would never wake up again. The death rattle as he breathed in and out was becoming louder. He felt like death warmed up. He felt terrible.

Blood pressure was dropping. It didn’t take a genius to figure that out. The blood was flowing out of the wound like a river moving quickly downstream. It was like a flood of rust coloured water.

He was dying. The blood pressure was dropping dangerously low. He hoped help would come before he died. He thought about Grace his partner in the force and hoped they could save her. He muttered something to the girl holding his right hand.

"He's got Grace."

"Who?" The girl asked trying to keep him talking.

"Damien has got Grace."

"Who is Grace?"

"My police officer partner. I see a light." The police officer closes his eyes and shudders.

"No don't close your eyes. I need you to stay awake for me."

"It's too late now."

The bloodstream stops flowing. The blood stops flowing through the wound. The police officer gasps once and lies still. He is gone now.

The girl sobs as an ambulance arrives too late.

First of November. noon.

Ryan Woods is called into the office.

“Sit down.” The boss Elizabeth Jean Mackay growls.

Ryan sits down on the chair. It is wooden, made of pine and black in colour. He is terribly frightened. What had he done wrong now?

“Mark Thompson is dead. He died at half eleven today. The medics pronounced him dead at the scene of the crime just half an hour ago. We have a grief counsellor on stand by in case you need anybody to talk to.”

“I’m ok. I barely knew him.”

“It’s there if you need it later on.”

"Ok."

Meanwhile Grace Addison was waking up in a dark room. The drugs she had been given were wearing off and she was beginning to be aware of the darkness and beginning to try and think her way out of it. Her police officer training was flooding into her mind. The first thing was to keep calm. The second thing was not to tell him too much about herself. The third thing was... She couldn't remember what the third thing was. Or the rest of the rules about engaging with suspects. Or anything about being kidnapped.

Damien unlocked the door and entered it with a loud creaking noise. The door needed oiling. He had a orange juice for her.

"Drink this. You must be thirsty." He said kindly.

Grace grabbed the orange juice and drank it quickly. It was smooth and easy to swallow. After drinking it Grace felt weirdly tired and lay her head back on the hard stone floor and closed her eyes.

Damien sat and watched Grace for a while. He studied the rising and falling chest of Grace as she fell asleep. The left boob was missing. He wondered. Why? Why was she missing her left boob. Thinking quickly he checked the right hand side. That boob was missing as well.

Why?

Quickly he put down his hand in Grace's pants. Was she male instead of female? Had he had a sex change? What was his name before? No she was definitely female! He found her womanhood and placed his hand in it.

Pulling his sticky hand out he sharpened his knife and grabbed his red scarf from the brown wooden hat stand.

It was then he found the lump in Grace's throat. Was it an Adam's apple? He cut open the throat vertically so he could cut the lump out. And saw... An ugly cancer filled lump the size of a golf ball near her throat.

Damien knew it was cancer. It looked like the lump his mother had in her throat. She had begged him to kill her.

Grace had never told anyone about the cancer she had been fighting for the past three years. She was a very positive and private person who didn't like to trouble folk with her worries. Secretly she had a lot of troubles. Her teenage son was in the wrong crowd. Her sixteen year old daughter was pregnant with twins. Her husband was sleeping with someone else. She didn't know who.

Damien knew. Her husband was sleeping with his would be wife and he didn't like it. Ok so they were not dating yet. But he lived in hope that Jennifer Day would become his wife one day.

Damien cut deeper into the throat.

Blood sprayed out.

Second of November. six pm.

"I found her like this in my garden."

"We have to ask where you were last night."

"In bed asleep beside my darling sweetheart Jennifer."

"Ok I won't ask what you were up to."

"I will tell you that we were doing it. Loud. Rough. Then slept well."

"Doing what exactly."

"You know. It. S. E. X. Sex."

"Ok you don't need to spell it out to me. I know what that is. Don't worry. I won't bother you again." Ryan Woods grinned sheepishly as he interviewed Damien Rice over the discovery of Grace Addyson's cancer ridden body with a cut throat in the garden of Damien's house.

Grace had a cross carved on the left side of her chest. She had been smothered by a red scarf. Her throat had been cut vertically.

"So I'm not under arrest then."

“No why would you be? You have been a great help.”

“I heard a noise and a scream then a groan. That’s all I remember hearing.”

“What was the noise like?”

“Like someone shouting help then being grabbed. I was in the middle of sex and didn’t think to help.”

“You wouldn’t think that. You are a great man. You probably thought it was kids messing about.”

“I did think that yes.”

“Ok. I have everything I need off you. Just sign your statement here and I will leave you in peace.”

Damien signed the statement.

“Ok signed it.”

“Thank you Damien Rice. I hope Jennifer is well. Did she hear anything?”

“No. She didn’t. She’s at work just now. She would have told me at the time if she had heard anything.”

"Ok. Nice talking to you Damien. Bye."

"Bye." Damien grins as Ryan Woods leaves the young man standing in a dressing gown and shivering with cold or fear. He had to be careful. Damien thought. He had to be very helpful to the police officers. One wrong move and it was curtains for him.

Just pray that they don't find out your secret. Damien thought to himself as he started working in his garden pulling up the weeds and dead flowers. When this was done, Damien started digging a deep ditch in his garden. He then grabbed the blood stained rolled rug and threw it into the ditch before covering it up and planting fresh plants.

Meanwhile Jennifer's parents were phoning the police. Their only daughter was missing and they were worried.

Jennifer Day always phoned her parents once a day at six o clock every evening.

Damien meanwhile was remembering the last time he had kissed Jennifer. She had kissed him back and... What happened next he couldn't remember. Just the warmness of Jennifer. The cold night. Damien taking Jennifer to his home. He must have been drunk. Yes. Drunk.

He pondered some more. Did they have sex? Did Jennifer Day stay the night? Did she go to work today?

Damien couldn't always remember what he had done. It was a result of the brain damage he had suffered as a baby. He knew that Jennifer had been angry. But why? Had he told his secret? The secret he must never tell. Never tell anyone.

The secret about his mother. A secret he knew.

He was the son of a rapist in the police force. And his father was Elizabeth's boss now. Damien thought he was safe.

The secret was that he Damien had killed his own mother. Murdered her in cold blood and buried her in the garden of her childhood home.

Gangsters used it now. They would want to dig her up.

Damien had to find her first.

Second of November. Half six in the evening.

Meanwhile the three police officers at the desk were not taking Jennifer Day's disappearance too seriously.

"She hooked up with a boy and won't phone you because you two stuck ups won't like him."

"Yip that's right Jim. What do you think Barry?"

"Yeah she is a bad girl alright. Steve."

"Jennifer Day would never do that to us. Would she darling?"

"No she wouldn't sweetheart. She's a good girl."

"I'm telling you two stuck ups that she has hooked up with a boy."

"Yeah. Missing person my left eyeball Jim."

“That’s right Steve. Cause you only have one good eye due to the robbery in the bank.”

“Got medals for it. Worth losing a eye. Barry go and get me some chicken nuggets and chips from the local cafe.”

“Ok Jim. What do you want?”

“The same.”

“I feel like a Beefburger and chips.”

“Aw Barry you have to be awkward.”

“Yeah Barry. Healthy eating remember.”

“Two beefburgers and chips.”

“Make that three.”

“What about us? Jennifer Day always phones us. Boyfriend or not she would phone. Something is wrong.”

“Does your daughter have any enemies?”

“No but...” The frustrated mother was cut off by the three police officers laughing at her.

"Go back to school mother." One of the three male officers laughed before heading to the cafe across the street from the police station.

Barry looked both ways before crossing the street. It was a one way street so he didn't need to worry about traffic. It was just force of habit. So he checked a second time just to confirm that it was clear.

He was a little bit shocked when a car drove towards him up the wrong way and he had to jump clear. He watched the red car motor along the road and nearly crash into a lamppost.

Barry forgot about his belly and started running after the car. He noticed that the registration number started with a HA.

"That's odd." He thought before the red Ford Escort drove away.

A black bag was thrown out of the passenger side of the motor.

Barry ran over to the bag as the car drove away faster than a bullet. He could see something inside.

He could see an arm as well as a hand.

"Guys there's a body in here. Help."

What they saw next made them lose their appetites.

Chapter four

Thirty years ago.

Johnny Button sighed and unlocked a simple door that had no windows on it. Alice Pidgeon was afraid. She didn't want to be locked up in the children's home. "Alice in here. I need to talk to you about your behaviour."

"I only wanted to know..."

"...Shut up and get in here now." Johnny growled as he turned the lights on and entered the room before pulling Alice Pidgeon by the shoulders in with him.

Alice looked around at the white painted walls and the four poster bed in the end of the room. The bed had crisp white sheets and a black and white diamond pattern on the duvet and pillows.

There was a tan, brown desk complete with black leather desk chair. Alice slowly moved to the desk. Johnny pointed to the bed quickly. Alice quickly followed his finger and sat down on the bed.

Meanwhile Johnny Button was closing the door. He then locked it. Alice Pidgeon was trapped inside the room with Johnny Button.

To the people outside Alice was getting shouted at in the soundproofed room. As far as Alice was concerned, she was being told to touch Johnny's face.

"Let's play a game. It's called the touching game. I touch you and you touch me. If you win you get a prize. Now touch my face."

So, she touched his face and nearly poked him in the eyes.

"Now you understand the touching game and how it works. I touch you and you touch me. Touch my face again." Johnny Button ordered. Alice touched his face again. This time missing Johnny's left eyeball. Johnny grinned. "Good. Now touch my nose."

Alice touched Johnny on the nose. Johnny grinned. "Good. Now touch my chin."

Alice touched Johnny on the chin.

Slowly Alice was pushed to touch lower and lower down.

Soon Johnny pulled his tight blue jeans and boxer pants down. Alice was urged to touch him again. Johnny liked forcing people to do things they didn't want to do. It gave him intense pleasure.

When Johnny had finished playing with Alice he pulled his pants and tight blue jeans up before buttoning up his shirt then gave Alice a packet of rolos and told her to be good. Alice was glad she wasn't in lots of trouble.

"Remember you can't tell anyone about this. Not even Joe. People will blame you for this if you tell them. It's your fault I had to do this. I had to punish you." Johnny Button grinned as he let Alice out the room.

Alice's favourite worker was Joe. Joe had white hair and green eyes and was always looking out for his charges when on duty. Joe liked telling jokes and making people laugh so hard they needed the toilet.

Knock knock.

Who's there?

Doctor.

Doctor who?

How do you know my name?

Everyone grinned and laughed at Joe's funny stories and jokes. He was a popular care assistant.

Alice loved Joe's stories of his childhood and adolescence. She loved hearing about the rationing that Joe was born under and grew up in. The blitz. The songs they used to sing.

"Who do you think you are kidding Mr Hitler? If you think we're on the run." Joe would sing. He loved the show Dad's army and remembered the local old guard helping him get home when he was two and a half years old. He also remembered the farm he went to when the children were sent away during the war.

He loved the cows, the pigs, the sheep and the chickens. There was a rooster called buck. Why it was called buck nobody knew. He looked after Barbara the sheep and missed her so much. She had died of old age.

He liked the pigs as well. He loved the bacon more.

Alice loved Joe and his stories.

Joe in turn loved Alice and wished he could adopt her. He loved the child Alice who listened to every word he spoke. She believed that he really had grown up in the war.

Joe told the truth and he wanted to hear the truth in return. Nobody wanted to lie to him.

Panto season came. Beauty and the beast was put on in the local area in the community centre town hall. It would start on the seventh of December and end on the nineteenth of January.

The children's home got tickets. Staff could and would come too.

"Joe." Alice asked. "Are you coming to the pantomime with us on the seventh of December?"

"No. But I'll be in later to hear all about it. That's next month the seventh of December, isn't it?"

"Its beauty and the beast. It's on at the local town hall. Not far from here."

"I met a beast once. He was a prisoner of war in my local town. Treguard his surname was. Can't remember what his first name was. Turned out to be a nice bloke. Used to give me his humbugs because he knew I liked them. He was called the beast because he was so strong."

"Wow. That's amazing. What happened to him?"

"I don't know. One day he just disappeared from the town. I never saw him again. I like to think he got married and moved away but the truth is he probably died of disease."

"That's sad."

"Yeah. But that's life. Sometimes life is sad."

Alice's ninth birthday came on the tenth of November nineteen ninety two and Joe and Tuesday celebrated with her. Joe gave her a doll that had a funny face and short blue, white and brown woolly hair. She wore a blue and white snowman Christmas jumper and white Christmas leggings with brown reindeer on them and red stripes on them as well as tiny green Christmas trees beside the giant reindeers.

I made her out of tights. My mum taught me how to make the dolls. I got the clothes for the Christmas bag." Joe said proudly.

"She's so cute. I will call her Blueberry muffin. She looks like a muffin."

Tuesday made Alice a necklace out of a few bits of wire, a stone, and some string.

Alice loved the necklace. She put it on every day and cuddled the doll every night as she slept.

Alice started to have nightmares because of Johnny Button's abuse.

She was a nine year old. Lost and alone in a maze of bedrooms. Johnny Button hunting her down like a child catcher in a children's movie.

Every move she made he was there blocking her. She couldn't escape him.

Every move. Terrifying. He even had a net to catch her in.

He would swing his net about and try to drop it over her head. That was how he caught you.

When and it was always when not if, he caught her, she would wake screaming.

She didn't understand the dream.

Time soon passed, a month went by, and it was soon nearly Christmas. Everyone was excited to see Santa and get presents from him. The yearly trip to the pantomime was fast approaching. In fact, it was here.

On the day they were to go to the pantomime on the seventh of December nineteen ninety two. Alice woke up with a cold. The doctor came and Alice was ordered to stay in bed. Alice fell back asleep after the doctor's visit.

As Alice slept the radio was put on. Joe would be in later that day.

As Alice woke up, she could hear the sounds coming from downstairs. It sounded like Joe.

"Joe." Alice called out losing her voice in the process.

Alice lay in bed stuffed with the cold and her head bursting. She listened to the distorted sounds coming from downstairs. She could tell it was the radio because Joe her favourite worker wasn't in yet as far as she knew. From the distorted sounds downstairs, it sounded a lot like Joe was talking to Judy Rabbit. Judy Rabbit was the boss, and everyone answered to her.

The sounds of singing were soon heard but poor Alice couldn't tell who was singing or why. It could be opera on the radio for all she knew. The voices of the staff muttered something to each other.

Alice Pidgeon closed her eyes and slept. When you have a cold, it's all you can do.

There were whispers downstairs. Does she know? When did it happen? Did he suffer?

The staff knew from the news that there had been several victims of a road traffic accident in the local area. A lorry driver drunk with tiredness had swerved the wrong way into a motorbike and half a dozen motors. The guy on the motorbike hadn't stood a chance. He had been beheaded so cleanly the guy was dead before he knew what was happening.

They knew Joe was driving a motorbike that day as he was the only staff member who owned a motorbike. Also, he was single and as far as anyone knew had no partner.

There was more than one fatality. The lorry driver was crushed between two cars. Of the eight vehicles involved there were eighteen fatalities. The pregnant woman was the only passenger still alive and had gone into labour. In fact she was rushing to the hospital with her now dead partner Frank Further.

Frank Further had suffered a head injury on the left side and front of his skull after the crash. It had killed him horribly and instantly. His head was caved in and his white shirt was covered in blood.

He was already dead. The shocked look on his bashed in face showed that.

As the policeman tried to keep the woman nearly giving birth calm, he noticed a phone ringing in the middle of the road. “Is this your phone?”

“No. I don’t know who it belongs to. Arrrrggghhhhhh. Think the man on the bike had it on him. Argggggh. Aaaaaaaaaaaaaaarrrrrrrrrrrrrrrrrrgggg gggggghhhhhhhhhhhhhh.”

“Ok dear. Stay calm. Help is on the way.”

“Bit hard to stay calm when you need to push. Aaaaaaarrrrrrrrggggghhhhhhhh.” The policeman checked the woman quickly.

“Oh my god. I can see the head. Ok breathe.”

“Just shut up and let me push. Nnnnnnnnnnnnnnnnnnnnneeeeeeeeeeeee eeeeeeeeeeeeeeeeeeeeeee

Aaaaaaaaaarrrrrrrrrrrrrrrrrgggggggggggh hhhhhhhhh."

"Oh my god! The head's out! Ok breathe because the shoulders are turning."

"Just shut up I need to push. Nnnnnnnnnnnnnnnnnnnnnneeeeeeeeeeee eeeeeeeeeeeeeeeeeeeeeee Aaaaaaaaaaaaaaaarrrrrrrrrrrrrrrrrrrrgggg gggggghhhhhhhhhhhhhh."

"Ok breathe."

"Aaaaaaaaaaaaaaaaaaaaaarrrrrrrrrrrrrrrrg ggggggggggghhhhhhhhh. Son of a... Aaaaaaaaaaaaaaaarrrrrrrrrrrrrrrrrrrrgggg gggggghhhhhhhhhhhhhh."

"Ok now we push."

"Nnnnnnnnnnnnnnnnnnnnnneeeeeeeeeee eeeeeeeeeeeeeeeeeeeeeeee. Aaaaaaaaaaaaaaaarrrrrrrrrrrrrrrrrrrrgggg gggggghhhhhhhhhhhhhh."

"And again."

Nnnnnnnnnnnnnnnnnnnnnneeeeeeeeeeee eeeeeeeeeeeeeeeeeeeeeee.

Aaaaaaaaaaaaaaarrrrrrrrrrrrrrrrrrrgggg ggggghhhhhhhhhhhhh."

A slimy baby boy pops out the mother. "Wah. Wah. Wah. Wah. Wah. Wah."

"Congratulations. It's a boy." The baby pees on the policeman a little as he wraps the baby in his shirt and hands him to his mother.

The baby boy pees on his midwife policeman some more emptying his bladder and cries vigorously "And he just peed on me."

As the medics arrive and deal with mother and son. Stuart, who is still on duty, picks up the phone lying in the middle of the road. The phone keeps ringing. Someone is looking for the owner of the phone.

The young mother names her new-born son after the policeman and it is also the second name of her partner Frank. The child's name is Stuart Frank Further.

Stuart feels honoured to have his name given to a baby as he answers the phone call.

Meanwhile at the children's home everyone tried to phone Joe. They had to know if he was ok. After a long pause a policeman called Stuart picked up.

"Joe Smith is that you?"

"No this is Stuart. Are you friends or family of the dead man Joe Smith? If so, I am very sorry to tell you that his head has been detached from his body and he was killed instantly."

"Yeah, we know a Joe Smith who rides a motorbike, and this is his mobile that we are dialling."

"He needs to be identified." The policeman's boss yelled grabbing the phone.

Judy took the details of where they were bringing the body to and hurried there at once. She had to know it wasn't him for Alice's sake. For everyone's sake.

The hospital was cold and white. The journey to the morgue was terrifying.

The morgue in the hospital was a very cold and frightening place. The white clinical walls shone brightly with frost and ice. The room was cold. It had to be. You don't want a rotten corpse before it gets buried. Do you?

Judy shivered with the cold. She hoped she wasn't coming down with something. That was all she needed.

The man on duty at the morgue was colder than his charges. His strict eyes darted around the room as Judy signed her name in the book.

His white hair, pale gaunt face and hollow eyes made him look like a corpse dressed in black. He lifted the sheet tenderly.

Judy Rabbit gasped and nodded at the line of stitching around Joe Smith's neck and sobbed slightly.

"Mrs Rabbit. Was he your partner?"

Judy shook her head. "Workmate." She sighed. "Alice will be broken-hearted. She has the cold, and the shock could kill her."

"And Alice is?"

"One of the kids at the children's home. She loved Joe. They were best friends."

"Alice will have to be told."

"Yes. She will. Just let her get well first."

The man lowered the sheet clinically. He had spent his life doing this job and it showed in his face. He looked almost like a vampire with his black leather jacket and leather trousers. His face was ashen white and almost blueish around the lips. His fingers were thin and bony.

Judy wondered how long he had been alive. Maybe he had been alive for a hundred years. He looked it. He looked like he had been alive for ten thousand years.

In truth he was nearly seventy two. It was his birthday on Christmas Eve.

Judy decided to get him some deodorant. The smell coming from him was like a corpse smell. Sweet and sickly with more than a hint of nail polish. She wondered if he had got presents from people.

"What's your name?"

"Edward Banks. Why? Who's asking?"

"We was mmm were thinking of getting you a gift for Christmas."

"Nobody gets me stuff. Got no family to care about me."

"We will send it to you later."

"That's nice."

"In fact. Come to the children's home and have Christmas dinner with us. You can visit us on Christmas Eve as well."

"Thank you." The old man gasps. Years being lifted from his face instantly by the mere mention of kindness. "This one will be buried before Christmas. I hear he had no family to mourn him."

"He has lots of mourners. Just no relations. He was gay. Long story short they kicked him out."

"Funeral is the seventeenth of December nineteen ninety two. Funeral home is sorting out the coffin and stuff. I hope you will bring Alice too."

"If she is better, than yes I will bring her."

"Good. My brother in law Henry will be in touch with you. Margaret my sister worked with him until the illness took her. Cancer, she had. Nobody knew until the very end."

"So sorry to hear about your sister."

"She died last week. My brother in law needs something to pull him out of his grief."

"Bring Henry with you."

"Great idea. I will bring him with me. He can dress up as Santa and I will be an elf."

"Perfect. The kids will love that. See you soon."

Judy then leaves and organises the staff and holds a meeting with them before telling the kids that are well the sad news about Joe.

Chapter five

Second of November. Seven pm.

The body was a woman. Half rotten but still recognizable as female. The hair was black and dirty. The skin mottled and falling off the bones. The heart full of liquid. The smell of death and decay. The softness of the body. The cancer in the throat and bones.

"The body must have been kept in a warm place." The coroner reckoned. "Or underground."

But how long was she buried for? The coroner couldn't tell. Just that she was smothered by a red scarf and had been dead for eleven years.

Meanwhile Damien hugged his red scarf. He should stop. Really. This never ends well. He had a drugged lady in his cellar. A dead lady in a far away garden. Several victims. He hugged his scarf again. It was soft and pretty. He got up from the kitchen floor, annoyed that he had lost his mother, then slowly went down to the dark and creepy cellar. He brought his radio cassette player with him and popped in a sixties cassette as he stood on the stairs. He pressed play as he reached the bottom of the steep stairs. He liked listening to music as he worked.

The young lady woke up as he unlocked the door. “Please let me go home.” She begged. “I promise I won’t tell. I won’t tell a soul.”

Damien grinned. “You’ve been a very naughty girl.” He answered before laughing loudly and sharpening his knife.

Second of November. Eight seventeen pm

It was pouring. Bucketing. Wild.

The old white haired man stood at the graveyard in his waterproof trousers, his Macintosh jacket and Wellington boots. He had his hood up and his umbrella had a hole in it. He looked like a old crabbit fisherman who hadn’t caught any fish. He felt like one too. He felt wet, crabbit and miserable.

He noticed the soil move. Slowly a hand appeared in drips and drops from the soil of the grave that had just been filled in.

“Blasted coffin collapsed.” He growled out loud to his underlings who were all trying to get under a shelter.

Suddenly a dead female appeared lying on top of the coffin. She was smothered by the same red scarf and had the same cross carved in the same place.

The old white haired grumpy man called the police. It was all he could do.

Second of November. Eight thirty two pm.

“Just got off the phone to Joseph King.” Elizabeth Jean Mackay growls to Ryan Woods. “Another body has just turned up at the local graveyard.”

“I thought that’s where bodies go.”

“This is serious. We have a serial killer on the loose who seems to be targeting mostly young women and girls. That's the sixth one. Not counting Mark. He is a different case."

"Is it possible that the cases are linked?"

"Mark Thompson was stabbed. The carvings only touch the skin. Not the heart. So no. They are not linked."

"Ok. Just wondering. You are the boss. I am just a rookie." Ryan grinned looking sheepish at his furious boss.

His furious boss for once cracked a smile. Ryan was learning his place. Just then one of the other officers knocked on the door of the office. "Freda come into my office. Ryan meet Freda. She will show you the beat."

"Hi Freda."

"Hi Ryan."

"I'll let you two get to know each other." Elizabeth Jean Mackay grinned as Freda and Ryan walked out of the office hand in hand.

Freda had dark hair and brown eyes. Her skin was like the darkest night. She was African American and had been named after the famous Queen singer Freddie Mercury. In fact If she had been a boy. Freddie would have been his name.

Her parents were big Queen fans and had all the CDs. All the video tapes and DVDs they could find. Freda was a Queen fan too. She had loved Gary Mullen on Stars in their eyes as a young girl. She was thrilled that he won.

Freda walked the beat and pointed to a old burned out house on the corner of the road.

“That’s where the murderer lived.”

“That’s my old family home.”

“You mean your dad killed those kids in the children’s home.”

“And the staff. I grew up in care. I am nothing like my father. I will not kill.”

“In the police you might have to.”

“I refuse to kill.”

“What if it is kill or be killed?”

Freda's words stayed with Ryan as she taught him the rest of the beat.

Second of November. Ten thirty-one pm.

Ryan started returning to the station. As he walked past one of the many council houses he saw a red haired man dressed all in black wearing a clown mask smashing into the house that he, Ryan, used to live in.

"Stop. Police. Freda, radio for back up."

"Ok Ryan. Just doing that. Zero Eight Oscar Four To base. We need back up. Man dressed in black with red hair committing a possible robbery. Need assistance please."

The radio crackles then Steve gets on the radio. "Zero Eight Oscar Four. Stay away from the house. Back up is coming."

Second of November. Ten forty five pm.

The man leaves. Ryan approaches the house. The smell of dampness and decay fills his lungs. He coughs at the second smell. Excretion of the human kind. The house looks lived in but stinks worse than a skunk. Ryan knew that someone had died here.

Back up arrived.

“He’s not there now.” Ryan roared to the three police officers that had arrived on scene. “Think something or someone died in this house.”

“Call the social security department to get it cleaned up.”

Ryan got on the phone to the social and told them it was urgent. He told them that someone had died in a house. Sixty three death street was the address.

The social security department told him they would come in the morning.

Third of November. Six am.

Ryan drove towards the house that he had left the night before at five minutes to midnight. He was tired and couldn't think properly. He drank from his energy drink can like a alcoholic necking a beer.

He felt like a beer. An alcoholic one. Not those non alcoholic drinks. He also knew he was on duty and couldn't drink on duty. It was a strange rule but it made sense. Police have to deal with a lot of stuff. Drinking alcohol would not help ease public opinion on the police. If anything it would make it worse. Public opinion of the police force was already rock bottom. The recent crimes against women were not helping the police make friends with the community.

Ryan finished the energy drink and threw it left handed into a open mouthed bin in the back seat of his car. The bin was meant to be for paper. Not cans. He parked the car at the space marked in chalk and got out the motor.

"Social work are just coming. You are in their space." His boss Elizabeth Jean Mackay grinned as the frustrated Ryan

Woods drove out of the space he was in before he quickly parked in the space just beside it.

Ryan opened another energy drink from his jacket pocket. He needed something to get him through the day.

The social work came with the fire brigade and the police battered down the door. The sickly sweet putrid smell of inside hit the officers gathered. Ryan vomited up the contents of his entire stomach. Others did too.

Flies buzzed around and there was spider webs everywhere. Not only that but beetles crawled the filthy rotten floor.

Ryan stepped on a wooden plank. It cracked and Ryan stepped backwards.

“Careful the floor is rotten right through.” Ryan yelled to the others.

Suddenly a cry of help echoed through the house. “Help me.” She yelled.

Ryan listening heard the sound. He quickly pinpointed where to go as the girl shouted for help.

"Help me. I can't wake my mum up." The small girl sobbed.

The woman beside her was dead. The six year old girl didn't know. Her mum was dead and would never wake up. The red scarf stuck in her mouth and throat had put paid to that.

The girl didn't understand what death was. She'd never seen anyone die before. Her wide eyes saw Ryan. "Are you going to kill me too?" She asked realising for the first time that her mother was dead and wasn't waking up anytime soon.

"No." Ryan answered gently. "I'm a good guy." He scooped up the young skinny girl and told her gently as he carried her out of the house. "You are a brave little girl. I wish I was as brave as you. What's your name?"

The girl answered. "I am Susan Smith. I was terrified. I hid. I'm not brave at all."

I am Ryan Woods. A policeman. You are braver than you think. Braver than you know. Smarter than you think. Being brave is not being unafraid. Being brave is doing the right thing when you are terrified out of your wits. And right now I am terrified. Terrified I might drop you."

"You won't drop me. I trust you."

As they got to the top of the house. Ryan got a phone call and gave the kid to the social worker. Another body had been found. This body was of a disabled girl with autism. His boss didn't want the case. The girl had red hair and her brown eyes were full of terror. She was left to die alone covered in her own bodily waste from her bowels.

The look of terror in her face was unbelievable. The police who were nothing more than chain smoking, coffee drinking, doughnut eating wankers both arrested and charged the innocent partner with her murder and sentenced him to life in jail. Even though the girls last words had been Chris he's hurting me they in their godly wisdom had decided that Chris was the guilty party even though he had been on the phone to her when it happened.

It was in their view Chris' fault. Not the other guy.

Elizabeth had a boss above her and he decided that Ryan was trouble. Chris was guilty of murder and possibly more than one.

The big boss decided that was it. Ryan was off the case.

Ryan didn't agree with the big boss. He didn't agree at all. Elizabeth had to agree. He was her boss and would fire her if she ordered Ryan to investigate. So she quickly and quietly took him off the case of the murder victims.

Ryan was not a happy bunny.

Third of November nine nineteen am.

Ryan walked into his bosses office. "Why am I off the case? I thought I was doing great."

"The big boss wants you off the case. You are suspended until further notice."

"But I wanted to catch him."

"The big boss wants to punish you for the manhandling the case. You are suspended until further notice."

That was it. No explanation. Nothing. Ryan was dumped from action just like that. Ryan had no choice but to go home.

Third of November nine nineteen thirty-one am.

The woman quickly runs past the bus shelter where the drunk guy is hiding. She is frightened of the drunk guy and tries to avoid his path.

Due to balance problems she nearly falls on him.

“Bitch. He slurs as he tries to hit her. Fucking bitch. He growls as she repeated the word sorry to him.

“Sorry my fucking ass.” He cries causing a scene in the bus shelter. Nobody cares about the lady so nobody intervenes. The lady calls the number nine three times hoping for the police to come.

Nobody comes.

She is only an off duty police woman.

She dials again and the drunk hits her drawing blood.

She tries to get away and the drunk goes nuts.

Blood is pounded out of her like a waterfall. When the drunk had finished with his prey she was on the floor bleeding.

A kind red haired man picks her up. Let me walk you home. He says gently.

She slowly gets up and goes with him.

Her body is found with a cross on her left breast and she is in a bin bag chopped up.

Chapter six

Twenty nine years ago

Alice slumbered on unaware that Joe was dead. As far as she was concerned, he was talking to her in her tiny mind.

“Joe. What is up?” Alice asked spinning in her dress knowing that Joe looked tortured about something.

“You look great as always.” Joe said grinning madly and in pain.

“Thanks.”

“I have to tell you something and you are not going to like this.” Joe answered gently.

“Tell me what?”

“I have to go now.”

“Why?”

“I got a new job.”

“What kind of job?”

"Army job. Soldier. Be away for a while. A long while."

"When will you be back?"

"Not sure. It's a long post in a far away place. I will come and visit you as much as I can. If I can. Ok."

"Ok Joe. Bye."

"Bye."

Alice woke up thirsty for a drink. She opened the door to her room and found an unopened bottle of diet coke and Sprite there. There was also a Victorian sponge in a box unopened plus a few packets of gummy sweets.

Alice ate the gummy sweets greedily. She opened the Victorian sponge and ate it all before drinking the bottle of diet coke and leaving the Sprite for later.

She took the Sprite into the room and sat it by her bed. She then closed her eyes and hoped to see Joe again.

As Alice fell back asleep, someone put the radio on downstairs, and Joe's favourite song came on the radio.

"Who do you think you are kidding Mr Hitler? If you think we're on the run."

The song played until the Mike went up. Joe King started talking.

"And that was for Joe Smith, who has tragically lost his life in a road traffic accident in the local area today. His workmates requested this song in his memory."

The next song played, and it was don't lose your head by queen.

Alice heard the song start and wondered why the radio was turned off so quickly.

"How inappropriate that song is. Someone should put a complaint in against him."

"Yes, that Joe King has landed himself in trouble now."

"I'll have his guts in a sausage casing."

"I'll have his guts for garters you mean."

"Yeah, that's what I meant. Just didn't know the phrase."

That wasn't the only inappropriate content that Joe King played on air that hour.

He played hold your head up high and losing my mind. He had been told the terrible details of Joe Smith's death yet still played those songs and don't lose your head back to back before talking to a health care officer about mental health issues.

He then made fun of the health care officer.

"This guy is going to get murdered one of these days if he keeps making fun of folk." The staff member who had been sent out to replace Joe grimaced.

"I agree." Groaned Johnny as he turned off the radio for the second time that evening.

The radio got put back on after nine o clock that night. Just then news broke that Joe King had just been sacked that night from Clyde three at half past eight due to low ratings. He said his goodbyes and left in shame at nine after taking the rip out of everyone he knew.

Everyone was glad to see him leave.

Alice slowly got better. She wasn't quite well enough to attend the funeral of Joe Smith, but she knew that he had died and attended his grave for the first time a couple of days after the funeral. She was told she could put anything on the headstone.

She put on the paperwork. Here lies our best friend, Joe. Sadly missed.

It was all she could say.

Everyone said it was a fitting tribute to him.

Christmas Eve soon came.

The nine year old Alice Pidgeon was surprised by a visitor on Christmas Eve.

"Santa's here." She cried. "And he has brought his favourite worker with him." Alice grinned pointing to a gaunt fellow with a red clown nose and a elf hat made of green and red felt.

"Hello Santa. The children are so excited to see you." Judy announced happily.

"And I am very excited to see them too. This is Edward Banks. He is helping me today. Be good to him. It's his birthday today. He chose to spend his birthday helping me."

The Christmas Eve meal was a party buffet, and the children, Santa and Edward ate as much as they could.

Then with full bellies and their thirst clenched. They listened as Edward and Santa read them a story.

The story that was read was the ugly duckling. Alice loved the end when he became a swan. She cried with happiness and shed a few tears of joy.

All the children got a gift from Santa. A simple doll made from tights and woolly hair, or a teddy made from scrap fur. Then the grown ups got a gift from Santa as well. They got a box of chocolates or a bottle of smelly stuff. Then Edward got his Christmas present of new golf clubs and Santa got one too. Santa got a new hat.

Then everyone sang happy birthday to you as Edward looked shocked and amazed at the birthday wishes and the enormous cake that could feed the five thousand that appeared in the room from the kitchen table.

Edward got after-shave and deodorant spray as well as a Halloween sign covered in fake blood saying, Beware. Bodies, in black paint. All and all he had a great birthday and promised to come back next year to read to the children again.

The next day Edward read them a Christmas story. They then sat down for Christmas dinner with Edward and Henry who when they were asked about Santa told the children. “He’s Henry’s cousin on the father’s side.”

The Christmas dinner was turkey with all the trimmings. Except cranberry sauce. Nobody likes it. Instead of the cranberry sauce they had gravy. There were mountains of roast potatoes and boiled carrots. Boiled Brussels sprouts and cauliflower cheese. Alice had everything except the cauliflower cheese. She had plain cauliflower instead. Alice hated cheese.

Afterwards they danced the night away then cuddled up with their new toys at night. Alice cuddled her doll and teddy.

Joe had made the gifts. He was the creative type. He would never be forgotten.

Boxing day dinner was interrupted by Edward who asked if he could come in. Inside his coat he had a special present for Alice. It was a pretty old doll made of porcelain and wearing a pretty red dress with dark hair like Alice. "She looks like me." Alice said shocked to see a doll like her.

"She was my sister's. Take care of her. I will be back in the new year." Edward said grinning.

He would be back to check on them next week.

On the day after boxing day Johnny Button told Alice that he wanted to play the touching game again. Alice didn't want to play but got up and followed Johnny when he told her she would lose her presents if she didn't do as she was told.

They went into Johnny's office. Johnny unlocked the door as always. Alice crept into the room feeling like a naughty schoolgirl. Johnny told her to put on her school uniform. Alice done so.

As Alice got undressed, she noticed that her chest seemed to be getting bigger. Alice put her school uniform on quickly and as she did so. Johnny touched her on the naked chest.

"You will soon be too old to play the touching game." Johnny told her.

Alice was shocked. She was even more shocked when Johnny forced her onto the bed and took her virginity.

Afterwards Alice felt cheated. She really had believed she could trust Johnny. She trusted him with her life, and he had hurt her. She had bled on the bed after he had torn her, and Johnny had been horrible to her. He had called her a cow. A slut. Said that she was his girlfriend.

Alice came back outside the room a numb and changed woman.

That night she had a nightmare again.

She was a nine year old. Lost and alone in a maze of bedrooms. Johnny Button hunting her down like a child catcher in a children's movie.

Every move she made he was there blocking her. She couldn't escape him.

Every move. Terrifying. He even had a net to catch her in.

He would swing his net about and try to drop it over her head. That was how he caught you.

When and it was always when not if, he caught her, she would wake screaming.

She still didn't understand the dream.

Alice's body started changing. She grew taller and skinnier. Soon she was five foot tall.

Weirdly enough Johnny stopped playing with Alice. She was too old for him now.

She still had the nightmares about Johnny Button.

It was when Johnny started playing with other kids that Alice whispered to a member of the female staff what Johnny was doing.

She explained what the room looked like and the rules of the touching game.

An interview with Johnny Button was made and it was conducted by Judy who took these claims very seriously.

Johnny Button denied the claims. He had to. His job was on the line.

It was then he told the group that Alice lived in a fantasy world. That she made up stories and lied frequently. He claimed there was no proof that Alice had ever been raped.

“Does Alice know what rape is?”

“No. She is living in a fantasy world.”

“And the boys? Are they living in a fantasy world too?”

“Alice told me that she that told them to say stuff.” Johnny lied hoping they would believe him.

It seemed to work. The staff believed Johnny. Judy wasn’t sure but had to go with her staff.

Alice was destroyed by the news that they didn’t believe her. They took her toys away and got her to work for a little bit of money.

She got fifty pence per hour. She also had to pay ninety two pounds a day for her stay.

Then to complete the punishment they burned her teddy and doll made of tights in the fire. They also broke the old red dress wearing porcelain doll into a thousand pieces. Alice was heartbroken. She wished she could leave the place and be a grown up woman, but she was still a kid and would legally be a child until she was sixteen.

Alice was fed smaller meals than her peers. She was not allowed meat or visitors. She didn’t have enough body fat on her to have her periods. Puberty took longer to complete.

Alice finally started her periods at sixteen.

The day before Johnny had raped her in her womanhood. The shock had caused the periods to start. Johnny's abuse had lasted years. She had never told anyone else about Johnny. Or the recurring nightmares.

She was a nine year old. Lost and alone in a maze of bedrooms. Johnny Button hunting her down like a child catcher in a children's movie.

Every move she made he was there blocking her. She couldn't escape him.

Every move. Terrifying. He even had a net to catch her in.

He would swing his net about and try to drop it over her head. That was how he caught you.

When and it was always when not if, he caught her, she would wake screaming.

She was ashamed and believed that it was her fault. The abuse that affected her trust in men. She didn't trust men. She believed they only wanted one thing. Sex.

The day she turned sixteen she was tossed onto the streets and told. "You owe us a hundred thousand pounds. Also you are an adult now. Go and get a job."

Chapter seven.

Fourth of November two thousand and twenty three. Nine am.

Katie Elsa Young walks into the office and starts looking at the evidence.

Elizabeth Jean Mackay growls at her. “I want this swept under the rug. Behave yourself and keep your nose clean.”

“Yes boss.” Katie Elsa Young answers. She has decided to put the blame on Chris.

Chris is charged with fourteen counts of murder and taken to see the courts in the morning.

Meanwhile Damien strikes again. He had killed yet another person while wearing the mask only to get a scar on his left eye for his troubles.

Tenth of November two thousand and one. Twenty two years ago.

The day Alice left the children's home was both the best day ever and the worse. Alice was scared. Not just scared but terrified. Alice felt like she would rather stand in a stampede of wildebeest then leave the children's home.

But leave the children's home she must. If only to grow as a person. You can't stay in the place forever.

The date was the tenth of November two thousand and one. The millennium year was last year, and everyone had been worried about the millennium bug. In Irvine a great thing had happened. The Big Idea had opened. It opened on the tenth of August two thousand. It will close after just three years of being open on the fifteenth of August in two thousand and three due to nobody coming to it.

Alice lives in Kilmarnock in Ayrshire Scotland and doesn't go to Irvine much. The staff in the children's home never took her. Alice didn't seem to have an interest in science stuff. But she had plans.

Big plans.

She wanted to get a job as a chef. Learn more about cooking. Make decisions about the menu. Serve customers their food. Taste exciting exotic food. Learn to put foods together to create meals fit for a king.

She wanted to cook.

She wanted to bake.

She wanted to learn stuff.

Did she have the qualifications? No. Could she get them? Yes. It meant finding a job and studying very hard. Could she get there? Yes, if the buses were running.

Luckily for Alice the local bus the x twenty five came on the hour but took two hours to get there to the college as it went around the scheme. There was also the number four that took her to Glasgow and the university she would have to study in was just outside the bus station.

Alice was excited. She hoped that she would make new friends or meet up with old ones.

She was so excited to be at college she didn't notice someone slip a few pills of something in her left jacket pocket.

"A gift for you. Take them when studying. It helps. Ask for Jack at the bike shed." An older teenage boy muttered in Alice's ear. He must have been eighteen. He was a third year student at the college and had nearly completed his degree in business administration. He knew how to do business alright. A few samples to get them hooked then cash in on their dignity. He was lacing speed with other bad stuff to make the speed last longer. Sometimes the speed lasted too long, and they died but there were always other suckers.

Alice had been given the drugs talk. But one pill couldn't hurt. It was just one tiny pill. What harm can one tiny pill do?

Alice took the pill and was buzzing all the way through the lessons. When it finally wore off Alice was exhausted.

Every day she took a pill. The buzzing took longer to kick in each time. Soon she was taking two pills. That got her going and buzzing.

Soon it took three pills. Then four. Then seven.

Meanwhile Alice was blowing all her money from her savings away. She didn't eat. She didn't sleep. She just wanted the pills.

It wasn't long before Alice had dropped out of college at eighteen years old and the only way, she could get the pills was by prostituting herself. She would sleep with anyone for the magic pills.

Anyone.

Tom. Dick. Harry. Bob. Anyone.

She done this for a few years. Then came a spanner in the works.

Alice got pregnant. She didn't know who the father was. But she needed a baby daddy. Mr Stephen Watt became the lucky fellow. I wouldn't say it was love at first sight on her side of the table. But he loved her and that was all that mattered.

It was a shotgun wedding with very few guests. Tuesday was there as well as some of the kids from the children's home. Everyone was so happy for the couple getting married. Even Johnny Button who stormed in the building drunk just to give his blessing to the happy couple.

After the wedding Alice told her husband everything about Johnny Button. How he had raped her and sexually abused her as an eight and a nine year old girl. How sexual abuse was wrong and that she had tried to speak out only to not be believed by the staff and she had been raped by him once more as a sixteen year old. The shock had started her periods. How the staff in the children's home had starved her to the point that puberty was arrested until she was much older.

She even told him the recurring nightmare.

"I was a nine year old. Lost and alone in a maze of bedrooms. Johnny Button hunting me down like a child catcher in a children's movie.

Every move I made he was there blocking me. I couldn't escape him.

Every move. Terrifying. He even had a net to catch me in.

He would swing his net about and try to drop it over my head. That was how he caught you.

When and it was always when not if, he caught me, I would wake screaming."

Her husband listened quietly then told her. "I love you."

Alice smiled. "I love you too."

This became their catchphrase that they said to each other day and night as Alice became free of the drugs. It was hard work, but she stuck to it.

Stephen Watt became the perfect gentleman and soon Alice was clean of the drugs. Alice started cleaning and cooking in the house. She was scared the first time she cooked chicken but managed brilliantly. She had learnt to wrap the chicken.

Soon the baby boy was born to the happy couple on the fifteenth of November two thousand and seven. They called him John Watt. He was drug free and happy. Alice was twenty two years old.

The nappies soon built up and the dustbin needed emptying a lot more. John fed well, slept well and well you know the other thing that babies do. Poop well. Soon John Watt became aware of his surroundings and started grabbing for stuff. He was a very curious baby. Alice watched him like a hawk. She had many sleepless nights at this time of her life.

The day soon came when John went to nursery for the first time. Alice met the teachers, and they seemed like friendly and nice trustworthy people. She hoped that she could trust them. She hoped that she had remembered John's milk. Phew she had. She had remembered her sandwiches for after her gym class as well which was a bonus. What she had forgotten was her water bottle for quenching her thirst. Luckily, she knew they sold water there.

Gym class wasn't far from the nursery. In fact, it was just next door to the nursery and in the same building as well. Lots of mums went there. Lots of dads went there too. Sometimes the mums watched the dads, or the dads watched the mums.

Sometimes nobody watched.

Today was one of those days. Or it should have been.

The first thing that happened when Alice got into the gym is that she slipped on the wet floor.

Nobody laughed and someone ran in to check that she was alright.

"I'm ok. Just a bit winded."

The staff fetched Alice a chair and helped her get into it.

"Thanks." Mumbled Alice feeling like the ground could swallow her up at any moment. "Was there a wet floor sign on there?" Someone asked.

"No." Alice answered gently. There had been no signage of any kind on or near the floor.

Only now did the wet floor sign come out. Alice relaxed as the staff bought Alice a piping hot pot of tea in a floral teapot with matching cup and not quite matching milk jug and sugar bowl. There was lots of sugar in the sugar bowl and lots of milk in the milk jug. The milk jug and sugar had on it flowers as well as the teapot. The cup had flowers on the handle and stripes on the body of the cup.

It all came on a floral tray that had bees on it. Alice felt very posh drinking her tea.

There was even a rich tea biscuit with it. Alice thought she was in heaven.

Maybe she was.

Alice was interrupted by a voice saying. "Mummy. I need a poo."

A two year old girl learning how to walk had escaped from the nursery. Alice laughed as the girl pulled her trousers down and sat down on the floor. Alice soon stopped laughing when she realised the little girl was pooing a giant poo on the carpet.

It wasn't long before the carpet had a huge sticky smelly poo stuck to it.

Alice couldn't help laughing as the little two year old girl was grabbed by her left arm and dragged away leaving the mess on the carpet to be cleaned up by staff.

"Jennifer Brown. We do the poo in the toilet. Not the carpet." The familiar man told the girl.

Alice recognised his voice. It was Johnny Button.

Yes, he was older, but his voice had a distinct nasal twang to it. She could pick it out in a heartbeat. She had memorised it in her brain and the knowledge that he was still working with kids was terrifying. Johnny Button whispered in her ear. "I can't wait to rape your son."

Alice was terrified and took out John Watt from the nursery with a mention of her fall. Nobody blinked an eyelid. Johnny Button was very popular with kids.

Meanwhile Johnny Button was entering his office with Jennifer Brown.

Fourth of November two thousand and twenty three. Five pm.

Courtroom.

The judge listens to the defendant. "Do you plead guilty or not guilty to fourteen counts of murder?

" Not guilty." The blonde haired man with blue teary eyes dressed in a suit and tie utters. He is innocent and he knows it.

"Guilty. Good. Lock him up for a whole life sentence." The judge yells loudly.

"I said not guilty." The man protests as he is lead away in handcuffs to the local jail.

Chapter eight

Sixteen years ago.

"We are going to play the touching game. You know how to play it. You win a prize if you do it right. I touch you and you touch me. Touch me on the face. Anywhere you like!"

Jennifer touches Johnny in the eyes.

"Argh. Not the eyes. Ok touch me on the nose."

Jennifer touches Johnny on the nose.

"Good. Now touch me on the chin."

Jennifer touches Johnny on the chin.

Johnny unbuttoned his shirt.

"Good. Touch me on the chest. Touch my nipples. Squeeze them."

Jennifer touches Johnny on the chest. She then bites him on the nipples and tries to suck on them. Johnny feels intense pleasure.

Meanwhile Alice had been persuaded by her husband Stephen Watt to report Johnny Button to the police. She was waiting for them now. The wait for the police felt like it was taking forever to happen.

How long would it take in an emergency Alice wondered. Would the police come more quickly if a masked murderer was on the loose? Would the police officers care about what happened to her? Would she be arrested for having sex as a child, even though she had never asked for sex in any way? Would she be in trouble? Would the police officers believe her? Will Johnny get away with his crimes again? How many others had he done this to? Could she get proof? Had he really threatened to rape John her son? Yes, he had. That bit she was sure about.

Did they know about the touching game? Was Johnny Button on the sex registrar? Probably not. Could they arrest Johnny

Button? Would they attempt to arrest Johnny Button? Would they even care?

Alice forced herself to keep calm. "Remember you are doing this for John to save him and other children from Johnny Button." She repeated the statement as a mantra. It was the only way she could focus on the task at hand.

The door chapped. Was it the police? Yes, it was.

The police chapped again. Alice hurried to let them into the posh and tidy living room that was covered in children's toys and books.

"Sorry about the mess." Alice apologized to the female police officer.

"It's ok." Annie grinned. "I have kids too."

"Kids can be so messy." Alice grinned sheepishly back to the female police officer and the male police officer. "I love kids that's why I must report several child abuses that happened to me when I was a child. The man involved is still working with children. I tried telling people in the nineties, but they covered it up and punished me for his wrongdoing. My name is Alice Watt. My surname was Pidgeon until I got married. I grew up in a care home for children. Pleasure something it was called. Oh, what was the second word again? Love. Beach. Joy. Zone. Pleasure zone."

"I know the place. Kilmarnock, isn't it?" The male police officer announced.

"Yeah, that's the one."

"It was creepy as hell." The male officer admitted to Alice as she tried to start calm. "Johnny Button done it to me too."

"He played the touching game with me. He wanted me to touch him on his face then moved down his body. I never understood how to play."

"He done that to me too." The male police officer gasped. "If you squeezed his balls, you won a prize. Still waiting on him giving me my prize."

"He never gave me the prize too apart from a packet of Rolos. I think he liked to abuse folk. He made me feel worthless. Like a piece of rubbish. He raped me as a nine year old and as a nine year old I felt betrayed by him and he raped me again at sixteen causing my periods to start after being starved by the rest of the staff. He liked power. He picked on the kids in the children's home because they had nobody to defend them. I had a recurring nightmare because of him."

The female police officer spoke. "You realise I am writing this all down."

"Yes. I realise that." Alice said bravely. "I wanted to complain before, but the staff never listened to me. They held a meeting and believed Johnny's lies. They then punished me for supposedly lying to them. And they didn't understand about the nightmares."

"That must have been very hard for you Alice."

"It was." Alice admitted. Tears starting to fall down her face. The female police officer fetched a paper napkin from her jacket pocket.

“Here.” She said softly, offering it to Alice like a tribal man offering a sacrifice to his gods.

“Thanks.” Alice said quietly with her hand out taking the tissue than blowing her nose on it.

“Feeling better?” The female police officer asked her.

“Yes, thank you.” Alice replied gently. She at long last felt vindicated in her suffering.

“We are writing this down as a statement and we will look to see if any more complaints have come through the system. If so we will arrest Johnny Button for more than one charge of rape and sexual abuse.”

“It was two charges. Right.”

“Yeah. That’s right. Two charges each. I’d lose my head of it wasn’t screwed on. Thanks Alice.”

“In the meantime, we will send out a police officer to arrest Johnny Button on two charges of rape and two charges of sexual abuse on a minor. And there might be a trial." The male police officer explained.

"Will I have to read evidence?" Alice asked.

"Only if you want to. It would help if you did."

Meanwhile the phones were ringing off the hook. A hundred complaints about Johnny Button had been lodged in the police system.

The police were called back out again.

The female police officer listening to the radio sighed. "Ok Alice we got to go and arrest Johnny Button. The phones are ringing off the hook. Seems it's not just you he attacked."

"I will read my evidence when we have the trial. I need to see him put away."

"I understand." The police said as they went out the door.

After they left Alice sobbed her heart out. Finally she could begin to heal.

Finally, she could grieve her childhood.

Her innocence. Her hurt. The betrayal of Alice.

Seeing him behind bars would help her heal.

As Alice went to bed that night, she had a weird dream.

First, she dreamt the nightmare.

She was a nine year old. Lost and alone in a maze of bedrooms. Johnny Button hunting her down like a child catcher in a children's movie.

Every move she made he was there blocking her. She couldn't escape him.

Every move. Terrifying. He even had a net to catch her in.

He would swing his net about and try to drop it over her head. That was how he caught you.

When and it was always when not if, he caught her, she would wake screaming.

This time she had a false awaking.

She then dreamt that Johnny Button was in her house and climbing the stairs quietly.

She was nine years old again. Alice watched from the door to her bedroom as Johnny Button went into her son's room.

"Let's play a game. The touching game. You touch me and I'll touch you. Touch my face John. I got your mother to touch my face. Good now touch my nose. Touch my big lanky nose. Good."

At this point Johnny's voice got deeper like a devil voice.

"Now touch my chin. Good. Touch my chest. Touch my fucking hairy chest."

Johnny rushed out the room naked shouting "Touch my balls. Touch my fucking balls or I will rape your mother."

John sucking his baby dummy touched Johnny on his balls.

At this point Johnny's voice became deep and slow. "Now John go and fuck your mother."

John refused.

Johnny Button walked over and fucked Alice in the womanhood.

Alice woke up screaming and dripping with sweat. She didn't go back to sleep. She read magazines and dealt with John the rest of the night.

Meanwhile Johnny Button was being investigated by the police.

The two police officers that had been to see Alice were quietly taken off the case for being too involved and two old men were added to the case.

The two old men had a stinky attitude towards women. Their view of women belongs to the nineteen fifties when men had all the power and women grinned and got on with it.

They made a hash of collecting evidence rather they sided with Johnny and viewed him as a pillar of society. They had a brief word with Johnny Button and were forced to arrest him to shut the press up.

Alice hadn't sold her story. Others had.

While in jail Johnny was sacked from his job. He was viewed as a danger by the children's care park and they wanted to avoid any confusion. They cared about children.

Johnny Button hoped that he would get back to the job that he loved.

Months passed. Alice Pidgeon started to heal. She trusted the police to convict him.

A year had passed since the case was opened and Alice got the trial date through. She got good news. She was pregnant again. The trial date was the fourth of July. Independence Day. She hoped it would be independence from Johnny's suffering.

Johnny hoped he would be able to convince a jury that Alice was an unfit mother. That Alice and the others were ganging up on him.

That Alice was deranged and stupid. That the others were in on his plan.

The time soon came when the jury had to decide.

Guilty or not guilty.

Alice held her breath. This was it. She could finally heal.

Alice wondered why the jury were taking so long to answer. Surely they had found Johnny Button guilty.

Of the one hundred charges of rape and the two hundred charges of child abuse. Do you find the defendant guilty or not guilty?

Alice Pidgeon held her breath. She could barely believe that Johnny Button was being jailed for the abuse he had put his victims through.

The twelve peers stood up. The foreman spoke.

Not guilty.

Alice was crushed. She felt betrayed by the police officers that had met her. She felt that she was worth less than a starving kid in Africa. She felt that she had no human rights at all. She roared with anger.

She was dragged out the courts screaming rapist and paedophile by her upset husband.

It wasn't just Alice who was upset. One victim remarked that she'd be better off dead. At least then the police would care about her.

After all the police were just only on the side of the criminals and not the victims. They were all coffee drinking, chain smoking, doughnut eating wankers who never caught anyone. Ever. Unless you ran a red light.

Johnny grinned as he spoke to the press and told them a pack of lies. He told them terrible lies, things about Alice that the press lapped up like flies around a corpse.

Alice went home crying bitterly. John asking mummy why are you crying?

Worse was to come for Alice.

Just after premature twin girls had been born to Alice. Stephen Watt found a lump on his left ball.

Stephen Watt without trying got Alice pregnant again.

The lump got bigger.

The twin girls got stronger.

The baby got bigger.

Alice got fatter.

The twin girls Agatha and Chrissy came home.

Alice went into labour. It was a tough delivery but after forty tough hours gave birth to a son. She called him Stephen junior.

Caring for three babies and a young toddler was not easy. Alice managed. She had to.

Stephen Watt became aware that his cancer was growing and finally went to the doctor.

It was too late. Too late to do anything.

The cancer was stage four. He had five weeks left to live.

Alice knew she had to care for him as well as the other babies. She owed Stephen that much. She owed him her life.

Chapter nine.

Fifth of November two thousand and twenty three. Three am.

As Chris stayed in jail. Damien got reckless. Damien knew he would be in big trouble if he was caught. He put on his clown mask and headed out of his condemned house. He was looking for the child. The young child had already escaped him twice. She must not escape him again.

Meanwhile Ryan Woods was looking for the girl Susan Smith. She had run away from the children's home and the police were doing nothing to find her. She was not their concern.

Ryan knew he had to find her, alone. He couldn't hope for any back up to arrive and he was bricking it with terror.

Would Damien kill him? Would Damien kill her? Would they escape him? Would he kill them both?

Ryan remembered that someone had told him that in the police force it might be kill or be killed.

Well if the choice between living and dying was killing that he would prefer to live.

Fifteen years ago.

Alice had the recurring nightmare again.

She was a nine year old. Lost and alone in a maze of bedrooms. Johnny Button hunting her down like a child catcher in a children's movie.

Every move she made he was there blocking her. She couldn't escape him.

Every move. Terrifying. He even had a net to catch her in.

He would swing his net about and try to drop it over her head. That was how he caught you.

When and it was always when not if, he caught her, she would wake screaming.

When she woke up. She realised Stephen was slowly dying.

And he needed her.

Stephen Watt became weaker and weaker. He struggled to eat and drink and he would paw at the bedding a lot. He also soiled the bed too. Usually wetting the bed in the process. There were times Alice would feel frustrated with him. But she always told him she loved him.

At last, the time came when Stephen Watt stopped eating and started sleeping more. He lost weight and his handsome looks faded into a gaunt hollow look. His muscles became non-existent, and his fat melted away until he was just bones.

Literally skin and bones.

At last Stephen Watt slept all the time and, as Alice changed a nappy on the youngest, her husband Stephen Watt stopped breathing suddenly.

Alice noticed the exhale and waited for the inhale.

She was still waiting five minutes later when the nurse came in.

“Oh.” Said the nurse. “I am not needed now.” As the nurse started phoning the doctors surgery to tell them of the death Alice sobbed and considered killing herself. She didn’t. Only because she didn’t want her children to grow up in care.

Alice put a box of memories for her to show the children when they were older. She then hid the box in the laundry cupboard. So, Stephen’s smell would rub onto it.

The children grew bigger. The twins struggled to walk. Alice started drinking. She had begun drinking the odd tipple to block out the pain of not being able to convince the jury that Johnny Button was guilty of abuse. Now she was drinking half a bottle a day.

The twins learned to walk. Stephen Watt junior learned how to walk.

The terribly twos came. Alice drunk more. John started looking after his younger brother and sisters. Winter came. John turned six.

Alice became a prostitute.

Alice knew her first day on the job would be hard. She didn't expect it to be this hard. She was wearing a black mini dress tied together with shoelaces and it both looked and felt tight.

To do this John had to look after his siblings. Alice felt alone and scared. She stood at the corner and stared into the darkness.

It was ten o clock at night and Alice was hungry. She hadn't eaten all day. She had only enough food to feed the children. They came first.

She felt her stomach rumble and was surprised. She then saw the black ford focus approach her.

This is it, Alice. She told herself. Focus. Focus on the task at hand.

The driver saw Alice and smiled. "Hi there. You must be looking for a customer. I'm your man."

“Yes, you are.” Alice said smiling grimly opening the door and climbing into the back of the motor.

The driver got out his car and climbed into the back when he paid Alice a thousand and fifty pounds for some dirty rough sex.

A thousand and fifty pounds would feed them all for a month.

He wasn’t the last. Six more paying customers came. Alice soon made five thousand and seventy two pounds. And she wasn’t yet done.

A final customer came just before dawn. He paid three thousand and fifty pounds. Alice gave him the best sex ever.

So, on her first day as a prostitute Alice made eight thousand one hundred and twenty two pounds.

Her second day was even better. She made thirteen thousand eight hundred and sixty pounds.

Alice took a day off to buy Christmas presents for the children.

On Alice's third day as a prostitute, things got weird fast.

Very weird.

Soon Alice was used to weird stuff.

Which was just as well. As Alice worked hard for the money.

The final day started normal enough. The kids went to nursery and school. They came home. They ate a good meal. Mum tucked them up in bed then went to work.

Alice pounded the streets and made fifty thousand then a final customer lured her in.

Alice walked over to the red sports car looking hotter than a fish in a flying pan. The man wolf whistled to her as she came closer to him.

His voice was higher pitched than most and he was not very responsible in using protection. He was young and foolish.

He was also very fertile.

After paying Alice a thousand pounds he impregnated Alice without a thought of her safety.

Alice didn't know until later that month. She felt sick and took a test then went to the doctor.

She was pregnant with twins. Twin boys.

As the boys grew inside her, the youngest son and two daughters grew too. So did the oldest.

The babies were soon born by Caesarean section called Richard and Dominic and Alice raised her little family.

Soon Alice fell in love again.

She fell in love with George Ball. In time they married.

It was a fake marriage as George was really a gay man.

Alice didn't care. She loved him. She loved him lots and lots.

Alice tossed and turned in the summer air. The hot stillness making it different to breathe. The heat was unbearable.

For Alice it was worse. She was dreaming.

A recurring nightmare. About him. Johnny Button.

She was a nine year old. Lost and alone in a maze of bedrooms. Johnny Button hunting her down like a child catcher in a children's movie.

Every move she made he was there blocking her. She couldn't escape him.

Every move. Terrifying. He even had a net to catch her in.

He would swing his net about and try to drop it over her head. That was how he caught you.

When and it was always when not if, he caught her, she would wake screaming.

George would cuddle her. That's all he could do. He was a stern man. Kind but stern.

He was the type who never wanted to disappoint his parents.

He would rather die first.

Chapter ten

Fifth of November two thousand and twenty three. Four thirty-one am.

Ryan Woods followed the unravelling red jumper. The girl had been given the jumper by the children's home and it was the one she was wearing when she went missing.

He knew if he found the jumper he would find her.

Meanwhile Damien was carrying in his arms something small and skinny.

It was the girl. He had Susan. Susan was fast asleep without a friend in the world. He had gassed her so she would sleep.

Susan's red jumper was totally destroyed.

Thirteen years ago

Alice slept nervously.

The nightmare again.

Alice tossing and turning.

She was a nine year old. Lost and alone in a maze of bedrooms. Johnny Button hunting her down like a child catcher in a children's movie.

Every move she made he was there blocking her. She couldn't escape him.

Every move. Terrifying. He even had a net to catch her in.

He would swing his net about and try to drop it over her head. That was how he caught you.

When and it was always when not if, he caught her, she would wake screaming.

This time he never caught her.

She caught him.

He ran. She chased him.

He ran faster.

Alice woke up. A false awakening. She dreamt that she was awake.

Only she wasn't .

She was a nine year old. Lost and alone in a maze of bedrooms. Johnny Button hunting her down like a child catcher in a children's movie.

Every move she made he was there blocking her. She couldn't escape him.

Every move. Terrifying. He even had a net to catch her in.

He would swing his net about and try to drop it over her head. That was how he caught you.

When and it was always when not if, he caught her, she would wake screaming.

This time he never caught her.

She caught him.

He ran. She chased him.

He ran faster.

She caught him.

Alice woke up for real smiling for once.

Alice fell back asleep listening to the soft summer rain on the windowsill.

She dreamt that her grandmother was cooking dinner.

“Gran.” She asked not realising that she was dreaming. “ I had a terrifying dream. I dreamt that you and grandfather died, and I was sent to the children’s home and was sexually abused by Johnny Button. The worse bit was nobody cared about me or listened to me. I had recurring nightmares about it and everything.”

“Sweetheart.” The grandmother smiled. “This is the dream. Johnny Button is real. It’s all true. We really did die.”

A clatter. A thump. A swear word. Then “Ouch.”

“There’s someone in my house.”

“Ignore them. They are not important.” Alice’s grandmother said gently.

“I can’t ignore them I have to wake up.” Alice said then woke up with a start. She listened to the thumping noise of shoes walking upstairs.

Alice turned to look at her partner. He was asleep beside her.

The thumps continued.

There was definitely, hundred percent someone else in the house. Alice was sure of it!

“George. George. There’s someone in the house. Get the mop there’s someone else in the house.” Alice yelled hitting George on the face to wake him up.

George yawned and listening to the noise answered. “It’s just the radio. Go back to sleep.”

“The radio is shut off and unplugged. I am terrified that someone else is in the house. Please go and phone the police.”

George slowly got up and grabbed his mobile. He dialled the number nine three times and asked for the police. He explained that the missus thought someone else had broken into the house and she was scared.

“There’s someone coming up the stairs. Please help. No it’s not the wife. She’s beside me. No it’s not the kids. They don’t wear size nine men’s shoes.

The phone hung up and a recorded message played. “Your call is very important to us. Please stay on the line and your call will be answered as soon as possible.”

While George yawned and listened to the message. The someone crept up the stairs and stood at the doorway to the bedroom.

The someone was a man.

They didn’t know him.

He didn’t know them.

The room went dark.

Alice had her feet grabbed by the mystery attacker. He tried to pull her out of bed. Alice fought back.

With all her strength she pushed his hands. His hairy hands away from her.

He grabbed her trousers and pulled them down. Or rather tried to. Alice's fat belly saved her.

Well almost saved her.

He tugged at the fabric stretching it out of shape trying hard to get it over her belly.

As Alice sighed with tiredness, he managed to brilliantly pull her trousers down to her ankles.

A deep nasal twang spoke. "Do what I tell you or the wife gets it. Put the phone down."

George put the phone down.

It's Johnny Button. Alice thought to herself in fear. It wasn't him. It was his son. Gary Lewis Button.

"So, the son shall do what the father did before me." Gary spoke bitterly before pulling his and Alice's pants down.

"I'm sorry." Begged Alice. "Please let me go."

Gary growled. “No! I cannot let you go.” He then grabbed Alice’s hair and forced her towards him making sure they connected like spark plugs on a motor.

Alice screamed in terror.

Gary started riding Alice fiercely.

Alice felt terrified. When would the torture end?

When Gary had finished, he spilled inside Alice and pulled his pants up and left the stunned couple visibility shaken.

George phoned the police back. Alice shook like a leaf.

The police took a statement and left. They had no intention of catching Gary Lewis Button. They liked his father too much.

Alice was told it was sleep paralysis. That the attack had never happened. She was told this by the officers that came to see her.

Only the attack had happened and left something behind.

Alice wasn't allowed to forget her attacker. Her weight gain put paid to that.

The child grew inside Alice. She hated the judging looks. The stares.

The twelve week scan should have been a joy. Folk saying it was her husband's. Others said she had extra martial relations. Still others claimed it was the devil she carried.

The doctor looked at the screen. Something wasn't right.

The child was not in the womb.

It was in the left fallopian tube, and it was ready to burst.

Alice was taken into hospital for surgery right away. She was not allowed food or drink and was booked in that day. It was important to remove the fallopian tube before it bursts as it bursting would likely be fatal to the mother.

Alice stayed calm. She trusted the doctors and nurses still.

She trusted the surgeons also.

"Scalpel. Nurse."

"Check." The nurse said giving the surgeon the scalpel.

"Forceps. Swaps."

Pop. Woosh.

The surgeon operated on Alice feverishly. The bleeding was bad and getting worse by the second. "Clamps." The surgeon growled not wanting to lose another patient today. This was his second case today. Alice was worse than his first. His first had bled out before lunchtime. This new case was worse.

Alice looked certain to bleed out before the surgeon could fix the torn fallopian tube. He had no choice. He had to take it out and stop the bleeding. It was the only way to save her.

Even after the tube and cluster of baby cells were removed Alice was still close to death.

The bleeding was stopped but Alice needed a blood transfusion of B positive blood.

B negative was all they had.

They took a chance and gave Alice the six pints of B negative blood. Somehow it worked and Alice stabilised. The surgeon finished the operation and closed Alice up.

“Alice is going to be ok.” George was told. They didn’t tell him about the battle to keep Alice alive. It was all in a day’s work.

Alice slept well and wasn’t aware of a thing.

When Alice woke up the surgeon was there.

“Alice. How are you? I was your surgeon.”

“Feeling better. And you.”

“I’m good. Now listen to me. We had to take away a fallopian tube as it ruptured. You still have a ninety percent chance of getting pregnant again with one Fallopian tube so you will need to take birth control pills for a few months while you heal.”

“Thank you so much for saving my life. I was sure I was going to die.”

“We treat these things all the time.”

“Thank you.” Alice said drowsily. She had a white blood stained gown on her otherwise naked body and a drip in her right arm giving fluid to her.

She also had a catheter inserted into her bladder. The rigorous pump emptying her bladder like clockwork.

George was waiting for her with the kids. They were thrilled to see their mother.

Unfortunately, Alice was too tired to see them. She slept through the visit.

The kids were disappointed. They really love their mother.

Alice was awake on the next visit that afternoon. The kids had made her a get well soon card. They then hurried to the nurses station to watch their favourite show Mission twenty one ten a game show that was all the rave at the time in twenty ten.

Everyone in school watched it. They all liked Caleb. He was friendly.

The kids were terrified of the robots. Alice wanted to tell the kids that there was worse things in the world than robots. Only she didn't want to take their innocence away.

It was then that Alice met Chloe. Chloe was one of the nurses. She was also Alice's younger sister. Their mum was still alive. Their shared dad Jack Peter Sparrow had died young but they always talked about Alice to Chloe as Chloe was growing up. Always.

Eleven years ago

When Alice felt a bit better, she tried to order tickets for the London Olympics that were happening in twenty twelve. Unfortunately, they were sold out. It was just lucky that her sister Chloe, that she had just met for the first time after her operation, had two tickets for the Olympics as she was volunteering as a first aid helper.

For Chloe being a trained nurse had perks at times. Alice was very happy at getting the tickets. It was something that Alice was wanting to do. Go to the Olympics that is. Chloe being able to get the tickets made it special.

Alice asked Chloe to come with her. Chloe accepted the offer.

On a rare day off for Chloe they went to watch the diving. Tom Daley was trying to get a medal.

As Tom Daley dived the first time with his male partner, Alice took a photo of him forgetting that the flash was on. A brilliant light came out of the camera and dazzled the pair as they dived down into the huge swimming pool.

Alice was embarrassed by her mistake and the worst bit was she had her camera taken off her and the picture was deleted from the camera.

Alice and Chloe were allowed to stay but without the pesky camera. That was staying in the office until home time. They were told to be quiet and behave like an adult.

Tom Daley got to dive again with his partner, and they ended up winning the bronze medal.

Alice and Chloe cheered loudly as Tom Daley and his partner got the bronze medal.

They then climbed out of the seating area and retrieved their camera from the office. Chloe was told to not bother volunteering here anymore. Alice was told to go home, and the pair were told they were barred from future Olympics.

Commonwealth games were not affected by the ban.

Alice went home with Chloe in disgrace.

Chapter eleven.

Fifth of November two thousand and twenty three. Five am.

Ryan Woods reached the end of the jumper. He found the last of it stuck in a branch with a note.

The note said I have her. Damien.

Ryan swore the fuck word and radioed for back up.

Nobody came. Nobody answered.

Ryan then realised that the radio he had was out of power. He was on his own.

Nobody was coming. Ryan would have to find her alone. He couldn't know if anyone was looking for him. Ryan dumped his radio and noticed some branches pointing westwards in an arrow shape.

"Clever girl Susan." He cheered as he followed the branches towards the Clyde. He will find her. He will save Susan.

Year twenty twelve. Month August. Date the seventeenth. Time three thirty. Eleven years ago.

Johnny Button was walking along the road. It was twenty twelve and Johnny Button was meeting with his girlfriend. His girlfriend sixteen year old Jennifer Property was bunking off the local school. She looked about twelve years old and was five months pregnant with Johnny's baby. She loved Johnny and called him her sugar daddy.

Jennifer Property was waiting at the strand for her beloved partner. It would be getting dark soon, and she was looking forward for going to the pub with Johnny Button. She would have a non-alcoholic drink of course. Diet coke was her preferred choice.

Year twenty twelve. Month August. Date the seventeenth. Time four thirty four.

Suddenly a strange man pushed past her. Jennifer touches his hands. They are hairy and covered in blood. Jennifer tries to catch the man to help him, but her left side feels wet and sticky. Jennifer touches her left side and feels a knife sticking out her. She screams for help but the stranger silences her by putting his bloody hands over her face.

"Sssssshhhhhhhhhh." The stranger whispered as Jennifer struggles to breathe through his fingers.

Jennifer gasps as she tries to take in air. Jennifer slowly goes down onto the ground. She can't breathe and is probably passing out through lack of oxygen.

The stranger thinks Jennifer has stopped breathing. He releases his grip.

Jennifer gasps once. She tries to get oxygen in her mouth and throat. Her throat feels very sore and uncomfortable. She feels afraid. She can't move much. She is afraid she is dying. She doesn't want to go. Not now. Not ever.

The stranger tries to shush Jennifer. Her side is drowning in blood. Her blood pressure is slightly low.

Jennifer tries to push the man away and run. She takes two steps before she collapses onto the cold hard blood stained ground. Jennifer is starting to feel light headed. The blood is in her throat now.

The stranger hears a voice and runs. Jennifer can hear but no longer move. She is too far gone.

Jennifer can't call out and the two drunk idiots walk by her assuming she is just another drunk woman.

It is not until three hours later that Jennifer is discovered lying on her side by two male police officers who assume she is a bit drunk and try to arrest her. She doesn't respond.

Johnny discovered her and found that she was dead and was automatically arrested by the male police officers that had been attending the scene. He was charged with murder. The murder of Jennifer Property. Her blood was found on Johnny.

Johnny is put into jail and left there until the morning.

When morning comes, he goes in front of an interview panel and is interrogated furiously.

Alice gets a phone call telling her of the news.

“Guess what.” Alice said beaming as she got off the phone to the police. “Johnny Button has been arrested for murder. Apparently, his girlfriend was murdered by him, Johnny button in a fit of rage last night at around six forty pm. She was only sixteen. What’s a sixteen year old dating him for I will never know.”

“Oh my god that’s shocking.” George said in a horrified voice. “Didn’t he abuse you as a kid and get off with it.”

“Me and several others.” Alice explained starting to shake with fear. “He could have killed me at any time, and they would never have blamed him.”

"I think its terrible that you have suffered because of him."

"I have suffered. Now give me a drink. A vodka and coke if you don't mind George."

"Just one. Ok. You can be a bitch when drunk."

"I'm your bitch."

"Alice, are you drunk already?"

"Yes." Alice giggles before drowning her face in a huge vodka and coke.

As it turned out a vodka and coke was Alice's favourite tipple. And not just one. She was drinking five before breakfast. Seven before lunch and ten for her dinner.

She was an alcoholic, and she couldn't admit it.

George divorced Alice in two thousand and thirteen. He had an affair with a schoolteacher and lost everything. He lost the home, the kids, and his dignity.

Johnny Button was jailed for twenty years for the murder of his girlfriend Jennifer

Property. It would have been a whole life sentence but the judge was kind to him. Johnny would celebrate his fiftieth birthday in jail and be let out at the age of seventy.

Alice struggled with the kids and became drunk more and more. Soon the kids were finding Alice passed out on the floor after another drinking session and looking after Alice. Making sure she had a bucket to vomit into. That she didn't choke on her vomit. That she drank water. That she ate. That she remembered to go to the toilet. So, she didn't dirty or wet herself.

And for all their help Alice drank.

John came home from school on a Wednesday to find Alice passed out on a heater on the floor with burns to her face.

John immediately called an ambulance. Alice needed medical attention. Those burns looked bad. Alice started to come to as John phoned the ambulance.

As Alice woke up, she complained of a sore head, so the hospital kept her in. They were worried she had brain damage when the truth was Alice was drunk.

A CT scan was performed. It was discovered that Alice's brain was normal. Emotionally Alice was a wreck. But her brain was normal. The only weird thing was that her brain lit up like a Christmas tree when alcohol was mentioned. Alice was an alcoholic.

Alice stayed in hospital for three weeks before the hospital let Alice out on day release. She was given a mental health team and told to stop drinking alcohol. Alice started therapy and talked at length about her problems. Her childhood. She was told to let it go. She was told to imagine she was holding a pen. Then to let the pen go.

Alice done the exercise many times. After each therapy session she would drink a vodka and coke. It was the only way she could cope with the trauma. The abandonment of her mother. Her grandparents abuse of her trust. Being a slave at eight years old. Being abused by

Johnny Button at eight years old, nine years old and sixteen years old.

Soon Alice was drinking during sessions. So, she was put on medication to stop her drinking. When she drunk alcohol she got ill. She would be sick and vomit. It was designed to force her to be sober.

Social services started keeping a close eye on the kids. Alice was afraid they would take her kids away. So, she started to behave. She stopped drinking alcohol. She started looking after herself and the kids.

Soon social services were no longer needed.

Alice Pidgeon started looking after her children and John started practicing other hobbies.

He tried kite flying but there wasn't enough wind. So he bought a toy airplane and started racing with it and doing stunts like dive bombing and loop the loops. Soon he was winning races despite being under sixteen. There was one race in particular that he really wanted to win. It was the flying squirrel cup.

Why was this cup called the flying squirrel you might ask. Well it was named after one of the best hobby flyers in the business.

Alice's grandfather in nineteen fifty two on the second of July had won the very first of the flying squirrel cups. It had also been named after his team. In fact he had asked to name the competition as part of his prize. He had won it every ear until nineteen seventy three when a newbie flyer had won the race.

John didn't know this about his great grandfather. Alice didn't know either. John wasn't expecting to win. He just wanted to have fun.

And they're off.

The race began and John picked up an early lead. He was stunned when nobody managed to get close to him and he made his way past the objects with ease.

It was no surprise when John crossed the line first and he immediately asked where are the others?

They were not yet finished. John had won the race. John was the new champion and holder of the flying squirrel cup. John was then told about his great grandfather. He was amazed that he was royal blood.

Well royal in the sense of a worthy champion in the championship.

Alice was so proud of her son. John was shocked.

John had won a thousand pounds in the race and with it being so close to Christmas it was a godsend. Alice treated her six children to the best that money could buy.

They had turkey with all the trimmings. A real live Christmas tree. John got an remote control aeroplane that was better then his home built one. He also got a hundred and thirty two pounds for Christmas.

Stephen junior got books and I mean a lot of books. He liked to read a lot.

Agatha and Chrissy the twin girls both got some fact books as well as the two biggest dolls in the shop.

Richard and Dominic the twin boys both big boats to play with.

After feasting on chocolate, sweets and chocolate oranges they tucked into dinner.

Dinner was turkey, roast potatoes, Brussels sprouts, roast carrots, roast parsnips, pigs in blankets and followed by Christmas pudding with ice cream.

At last they were all stuffed. The leftovers were saved in the fridge. Not that there was many leftovers. The kids were so hungry and the food was delicious and to die for.

The best bit was when Edward visited. Alice hugged him.

It was the last time they would meet up.

Chapter twelve

Fifth of November two thousand and twenty three. Four Forty five am.

Damien sharpened his knife on his stone as the girl, Susan, woke up.

“You are the man who killed my mother.” She says shocked to see his clown mask still on him.

“Shut up or you are next.” Damien growls.

The girl screams then shouts. “Help.”

Damien swears again.

Third of January two thousand and nineteen. Four years ago.

Edward died on the third of January in two thousand and nineteen. He was very old. A hundred and two.

Alice attended the funeral with her children. They had loved the old man very much.

The funeral was full of mourners all talking about the dead man's good deeds. Everyone was shocked that he had passed so soon after Christmas. Alice knew it was bitterly cold and that the cold could give someone a heart attack.

What nobody knew was that he had left Alice and her family a hundred thousand pounds in cash. Alice could at long last set up her cake baking company. She called it Baked Cakes.

It was a roaring success. Alice soon had a secure business account and she earned thousands a week. Hundreds a day.

The kids studied as Alice took orders from people and baked them.

That was how she met her mum.

Her mum Grace ordered a cake to celebrate her birthday and Alice made sure it was a nut free chocolate orange cake with candied orange slices on top.

Grace loved the cake and was proud of her daughter. Then they got more good news.

Johnny Button had hanged himself in shame. His death was termed a suicide and he was buried in the prison yard with only the prison guards watching.

Alice started drinking again. Only way she knew to blot out the pain.

At first she was drinking a bit. Then a lot.

The final straw came when she lost her driving licence for being drunk.

Not only that but she had to pay a fine of sixty pounds and another five thousand pounds in court fees and she lost her driving licence in the courts.

Being drunk in court didn't help. Calling the law an ass really didn't help. Calling the judge an idiot made him put her in jail for a month.

With no driving license she had to sell the business. It was a terrible thing as it made the children homeless on a technicality. She had set it up in the house.

Luckily Grace had plenty of room so Alice and the children started with her for a few months.

That Christmas there was one gift each around the tree for everyone. They all got the same. A jumper and furry socks.

Dinner was beans on toast and the children were starving hungry the next day.

Alice was definitely going to rebuild the business next year. She rented a flat and started learning about businesses.

Then a terrible disaster happened. COVID nineteen.

The year started good enough. Alice put in a application to start a business. The children studied hard.

Then COVID nineteen hit the UK and everything went into lockdown.

No business was allowed to open unless they were essential. Alice's cake business died a death.

The kids went to school on zoom. Luckily the school provided the laptops.

Alice felt more alone than ever.

Alice's mum Grace tried to hook Alice up with a black haired man who wore a Def leopard t shirt and blue jeans with safety pins in them. He looked like he was in his fifties. Way too old for Alice. Yet Grace said that he was a gentleman.

They met online for the first time on the tenth of April as everywhere was still shut. They shared virtual dates and chatted about their interests to each other.

It was the twenty second of July when they met in person wearing a face mask. Alice was wearing a flowery dress with a red rose on her white face mask.

Tom was wearing a black face mask with a skull on it topped with a iron maiden t shirt and blue jeans with safety pins in them.

The first thing Alice noticed was how busy the bus station was. It was mobbed.

Alice loved Tom so much.

The best bit was he loved her too.

They had drinks and dinner then headed home. Alice was so happy. As time past the two of them got closer and closer.

“I love you, darling.”

“I love you too, angel.”

“I love you more, darling.”

“No, I love you more, angel.”

“Mum, dad, you two are embarrassing us. Just kiss and say goodnight already.”

“Goodnight my darling sweetheart and handsome fella.”

“Goodnight my beautiful angel of the north.”

“Mmmmmmmmmmmmmmmmmm ooo.”

“See you next week.”

“Yes, see you next week.”

“Mum that was embarrassing.” John groans as Alice kissed her man Tom again.

Grace looked at her daughter proudly. “Alice I picked you a good one. Let’s hope you keep him.”

“I will try my very best to keep him mother. I know it’s not easy keeping a man. I loved Stephen and he died of cancer. Don’t let him go is my motto.”

“What about George?”

“He had an affair. I divorced him.”

“Did you keep your money?”

“Mother I got his money.”

Twenty third of July Twenty twenty. Three am.

Alice thought nothing more of the conversation she had had with her mother. But that night she dreamt a weird and unsettling dream.

Tome was in her grandmother’s grave.

“Tom what are you doing in my grandmother’s grave?

Tom grinned while covered in soil and digging with his hands. “Looking for you.” He answered.

Alice woke up screaming.

Just then Alice got a phone call. Tom had crashed his motorbike. The worse bit was he was having CPR done to him.

While on the phone Alice was told. They're calling it. He's dead.

Chapter thirteen

Fifth of November two thousand and twenty three. Four Forty five am.

Ryan Woods swore that he would find the girl. Then he heard a scream.

It was the girl. Susan.

Ryan heard a yelp of help and his heart stopped.

Damien had her. Damien was desperate to keep a hold of the girl. “Scream again and I kill you.” He told Susan.

Susan started a scream and Damien clapped his hand on Susan’s mouth.

Ryan heard it and sprinted westbound. He grabbed Damien and pinned him to the floor. “Susan run.” Ryan yelled fighting Damien’s attempt to get up with all his strength.

Susan took the hint and ran. She was a smart kid. It wasn’t long before she ran into

Elizabeth Jean Mackay, who was looking for Ryan to tell him that Chris had been released from prison on a technical note. He had not been given a trial and evidence had proven his innocence.

"Damien got man back there. Damien got Ryan. Damien got knife. Policeman Ryan in danger." Susan gasped running for her life. Elizabeth hugged her and radioed for backup. "They were west." Susan gasped pointing backwards trying to get her breath back.

Elizabeth Jean Mackay knew that west headed to the Clyde.

The only things there were a catholic chapel and a red metal bridge. The red metal bridge had bits of gold paint on it and it looked very stunning. It was also old and cold.

The Clyde bubbled inevitably. It looked inviting and you would be forgiven for wanting a dip. The water was very cold and you would be freezing cold if you tried.

Ryan was shocked that Damien had taken his clown mask off that was hiding his fresh scar and placed it on the bridge, where the passers by walk, and that Damien wanted to fight him standing on the top of the bridge. You would have to be drunk to fight him. The guy was holding a knife for Christ sake. You would have to be insane to fight on a rickety old bridge like that.

Couldn't Damien just, you know, surrender like normal people.

Damien grabbed the cold metal and he placed a foot on the slippery bridge.

"Don't" Ryan warned. He knew it was dangerous.

Damien bit his knife and pulled himself up. With the knife between his teeth Damien climbed up the bridge to the top of the metal frame.

Ryan Woods followed him cautiously. His belt dangling dangerously low.

The pair of them trying to keep their balance as they stood on the thin metal on the top of the bridge.

Ryan had tucked his thumb into his other hand as he had been trying to keep warm pulled out his thumb from his other hand and yelled. “I declare a thumb war.”

Damien laughed and put his knife away in his jacket pocket. “I accept your duel. Just let me get closer.”

“OK. Let’s do this.” Ryan grinned trying to stay upright in the circular part of the bridge.

The pair started to duel with their thumbs while standing on the top of the metal bridge. “Thumb war to the death.” Damien cheered.

“Now steady on.” Ryan remarked but it was too late. Damien stabbed Ryan Woods in the chest.

“Ouch. I’ve been stung.” Ryan yelled as Elizabeth Jean Mackay watched from a distance.

As Damien stabbed Ryan and pulled the knife out. The backwards movement meant he slipped, lost his footing and fell backwards grabbing the bridge as he fell.

Ryan laughed when he saw the blood pouring from him. “I win Damien. You cheated. You used a knife. Silly billy.”

“The name is Damien.” Damien roared.

“Let me save you Damien. My name is Ryan. I want to help you.” Ryan begged.

Damien looked visibly pained. “No. Never!”

Ryan tried to grab him to save him but it was too late. Damien lost his grip and fell backwards off the bridge, like a lion falling off a cliff, and disappeared into the water.

Damien gasped popped his head up briefly and yelled. “I can’t swim.” The current then dragged him down like a horse sinking into quicksand.

Ryan watched the water for a while. Nobody came up for air.

Elizabeth, carrying Susan on her shoulders, patted Ryan on the shoulder. “Let’s go.”

Ryan showed his bloody chest to Elizabeth. “He stabbed me.”

Elizabeth called an ambulance for Ryan.

Ryan was in a bad way. Susan was sure he was going to be ok.

"He's going to be ok. Right?" Susan asked Elizabeth as Ryan passed out from the pain

"Men are big babies Susan." Elizabeth Jean Mackay grinned. "Ryan I want you back on duty tomorrow."

Chapter fourteen

Feb the fourteenth two thousand and twenty three. Four am.

There is an ugly looking man standing by a bus stop in the dark night dressed in black and wearing a policeman’s hat. He is dressed up for someone’s birthday and wants some action.

The man grabbed Alice by the hair and dragged her to an alleyway near hope street in Glasgow. There is a pub nearby. The pub is busy. People are in it drinking and yelling songs. Alice is amazed when the man gives her three thousand pounds. He then tells her to take her trousers and knickers off or he will kill her horribly.

Alice is forced to do as he says. Alice is afraid for her life.

He bends her over on a parked car and forces himself inside her.

Alice is terrified. She thinks he is going to kill her.

After a awful five minutes the man pulls out all sticky then pulls his pants and trousers up. Alice is left terrified and trembling with fear. She doesn't know it but he has left something inside her.

HIV.

HIV can be treated with medication. One pill stops the virus from being passed on. You can live an normal life.

Alice didn't know she had HIV for six months. HIV does that. It hides. It lurks. It destroys slowly.

When she found out on the Saturday after she had got drunk and attacked a disabled girl in Glasgow Buchanan bus station and Chloe took her to a private hospital to get tested, she knew she had to report the terrible rape to the police.

The police laughed at her and told her not to be stupid. That she didn't have HIV. That she was a time waster and was lucky not to be arrested for wasting police time.

This eventful day had happened just the day after she had attacked, while drunk as a sunken sailor, a disabled girl who was only pointing out what everyone else was thinking.

Alice was drunk and was wanting more alcohol. She figured the disabled girl was a softy. She saw how she felt safe with her disabled partner and pounced.

The drunk woman approached the red haired girl.

“Is there alcohol in that? Give me a drink. I’ll bet there’s alcohol in that bottle of diet coke you have there. Come on i’m dying for a drink.”

“No. There’s not any Alcohol in it.” The red haired girl with autism wearing a pink jumper and black trousers on explained or tried to. “It’s non alcoholic. It’s just diet coke with the lid torn off to make sure it shuts properly.”

“There’s got to be alcohol in it. You are drinking alcohol in public and I want it.”

The red haired girl remembered what had happened last time she had surrendered her juice to a drunk person.

They had taken one sip of it and poured it all out on the pavement complaining that there was no alcohol in it.

She didn't want to lose her juice so repeated for a third time that the juice had no alcohol in it. She turned to her partner and starting to explain to the blond haired disabled man why you don't give your juice away to strangers who look like drug users or drunk casually started with.

"She might have Aids."

Four little words. The woman heard.

Might was the word she didn't hear.

Alice swore.

"You bitch. You fucking cheeky bitch. Saying I have aids."

"I said you might have aids." The girl tried to explain. If given the chance she would have explained that she couldn't give her the juice for hygiene reasons. That she was disabled and could ill afford to catch nasty germs off a strange person.

Alice never gave the girl a chance.

Alice drunkenly punched the girl in the forehead causing the girl to immediately apologize and attempt to explain that she had autism.

"Cheeky bitch. I'll knock your fucking block off. I'll separate your head from your fucking body." Alice roared as the girl ran off visibly shaken with her partner.

Chloe grabbed Alice and roared. "You stupid bitch. She's fucking autistic. Come home and sober up before you get arrested."

Alice reluctantly went home. John was looking after the other kids.

Alice slept for a time and could remember fuck all when she woke up the next day.

Chloe filled her in.

"You drunk attacked a disabled girl. You really need to sober up. Mum's got the kids. You must get tested for stuff and HIV and get dry. Then you will get them back. The social say you won't keep them if you get drunk again. There's this camp that dries alcoholics up. You are booked in for the fifteenth of November for a month."

"That's John's birthday. The fifteenth."

"I don't care. You can see him on the tenth."

Seventh of November two thousand and twenty three. Nine fifteen am.

The divers dived into the Clyde.

Ryan watched the action, covered on his chest were lots of bandages. Susan was back in the children's home as if nothing had happened. Kids were tough.

Ryan scanned the water nervously as the divers searched for the body. Damien was dead. He had to have been. Damien must be a goner. There was no way he could have survived the fall into the Clyde.

The red metal bridge stood as a witness to that. The clown mask lay on the bridge as a memory of danger.

“He’s dead isn’t he Elizabeth?”

“Looks like it Ryan. I’m sorry I didn’t help you fight him.”

“It’s ok. You were trying to save the child.”

“You saved her. I just picked her up.”

“I hope she will be ok.”

“She will be. I am sure of it. She is a tough little mite.”

The divers surface. No. Nothing. Must have washed out to sea.

The truth is far more sinister.

Chapter fifteen

Tenth of November two thousand and twenty three. ten am.

As I sat waiting for Chris sitting on one of the seats in the bus station somewhere between the statue of the two lovers and the big fancy clock, I noticed a man looking odd.

The man at first glance looked like a father to be waiting for a birth. His striped grey and black polo shirt hidden under his black hoodie jacket make him look at odds in the bus station. They didn't match his dirty blue jeans. His short styled straight red hair was puffed up on his head and his red Hitler moustache was connected to his bushy red beard and made him look like a leprechaun. His blob nose and the fact his eyes darted from left to right as well as the fact that he was chewing gum furiously showed me that he was tense. Very tense. He had his hands in his pockets and was pacing the floor. I noticed as he paced that he had a white scar on the back of his head like a comma. His thick bushy eyebrows and his huge sticky out ears like king Charles made him look ugly. His jeans didn't match the black Nike air trainers he was wearing. The trainers had a white tick on them.

I wondered where I had seen him before. Maybe on a wanted poster.

I looked away as he glared at me. Someone came over to him. I didn't see who just a blur of yellow hair wearing a red dress but by the time I glanced his way again properly he was gone and the someone else was with him.

I hoped that he had a first date and was not the slasher that I had heard about.

The famous slasher was always wearing a mask. A single silly clown mask. He also wore an apron over his black coat and wore on his feet black Nike air trainers with a white tick.

Trainers just like those ones.

Surely not. He didn't look the type. Did he?

I had checked for blood on the trainers but I was too far away to see any visible blood.

It didn't mean that they were clean.

Also, blood doesn't show much on black. Try having a bloody nose at work once and you will see what I mean.

I breathed a sigh of relief as the man left and breathed another sigh of relief when my darling sweetheart Chris Morgan comes near me.

"Hi Chris." I purr to my darling sweetheart as he kisses me.

"Hi Elizabeth" He grins back. He sounds sexy.

I feel sexy.

Our date goes well and we have a wonderful time eating brunch in Glasgow.

I get back home in time to see the six-o clock news. The other someone comes on screen. She is blonde haired and blue eyed wearing a red dress and red shoes.

Her name is Janice Alice Martin. She is nineteen years old.

She was missing. It wasn't like her to go missing. Her parents put an appeal for information.

She was last seen at ten am.

The time I saw her leave with the man.

A number comes on screen and people are urged to call if they have information about the case.

I phone the number. "Police please."

A policewoman answers.

"Hello." She sighs.

I start talking.

As I talk a builder works tiding up the building site in wild and windy weather. As he works, he feels a hand tap him on the shoulder. He looks behind him and sees a single silly clown mask.

He is terrified of clowns.

“Ha ha very funny, if you are five. Come out. Come out where ever you are.”

Nothing replies to his plea.

“It’s not funny man. I am bloody terrified and you know it.”

The scaffolding falls and he is taken from behind.

He struggles to break free. The black blob with the green eyes takes him before the scaffolding breaks down and the storm gets stronger.

The black blob grabs the clown mask and flees.

Before he leaves, he cuts a deep scar in the shape of a cross on his victim’s left breast.

The slasher has stuck again.

I finish talking and hang up.

The bleeping starts on the builder’s phone. His second job is calling.

The patient is crashing on the operating table.

The surgeon is nowhere in sight. The storm outside gets stronger. The trainee surgeon tries to save him.

The storm gets worse. The trainee surgeon starts CPR. The nurses' empty vials of blood as a young police officer watches in horror.

"He will be all right boss. Won't he?" She says tears falling from her eyes.

"He has to be." Her boss says grimly. "You are not allowed to die at work. Ricki said so. Also, you must be at work for twenty four hours a day if you are the police. Ricki says so."

The police officer nodded. She knew the prime minster Ricki Sinak had made this law only last week. She also remembered that she was lucky to be alive today after facing the robbery that had went wrong and the gun being fired. Her co worker had taken the bullet. The bullet that had been meant for her. Her co worker had been two days away from getting a nice cosy desk job instead of being out there finding the needle in the haystack that was the slasher.

The slasher. That was what the press had dubbed him. That is if he was a male. For all they knew he could be a woman. The victims were all different but had one thing in common. They all were women. All from the area of Glasgow and surrounding areas. Like Paisley and North Ayrshire to name but a few. Some gay. Some straight. Some black. Some white. Some of Asian descent. Some African.

One sixteen year old. The third youngest of the victims so far was twenty-three and a chemist. Blonde but smart enough to hand meds out without making mistakes.

You have to be very smart to hand meds out. Genius level smart. Not Garnock Academy level which is one level above stupid.

The police officer sobbed as the nurses covered the man. They had tried and failed to save him.

The storm died down.

The police were called out again. The police officer and her boss stayed at the hospital and stayed with the family as they were told the bad news. The police officer was then sent to catch the robbers that had killed her partner Martin Alan Peters.

The date changed from the tenth of November two thousand and twenty three to the eleventh of November two thousand and twenty three. It was 00.00.00 am. A second later it was 00.00.01. The police officer got in the car and sat there. She sobbed bitterly and furiously into the steering wheel.

“Why must you die Martin?” She sobbed. Honking the horn in anger while tears flooded her cheeks.

She didn’t know how long she had sat there. But the dawn starting to break disturbed her.

She became aware of the swallows and the sparrows as well as the crows, seagulls, doves and the quiet cooing of the pigeons. The tears still fell.

Then there was a tap on her window. She turned to her right, saw a pregnant woman wearing an oxygen mask on her face and a red dress and rolled down the window.

"Can I help you miss?" She asked before feeling blood dripping down her back. She turned around and saw a clown masked black clothed figure running away empty handed. "Help" She shouted before passing out. As she passed out, she noticed she was in a parking spot for nurses. She had seen it but as she was police, she had thought it was ok to park there. She hadn't locked the door of her car. She begged to live as the darkness took her.

Bleep. Bleep. The heart monitor bleeped loudly. The sound of air rushing into a mask was reassuring. The gentle breaths in and out meant one thing.

She was alive.

She remembered the Nike trainers. She remembered the clown mask. But not much else.

It wasn't surprising really. She had been dead for twenty minutes. They had nearly given up on her.

She didn't know that. Just knew she had been dreaming. Dreaming about God. Dreaming that she was dead. She had dreamt she was in heaven with her partner Martin.

She tried to move but couldn't. She seemed to be strapped down.

The needle went in. She fell into a deep dreamless sleep.

At zero seven hundred hours two minutes and nine seconds on the eleventh of November two thousand and twenty three Katie Elsa Young was put into an induced coma after being attacked in the hospital car park in the nurse's parking bay just before dawn.

Her workmates tried to find the attacker.

Eleventh of November two thousand and twenty three. Two thirty two am.

The attacker was waiting for the bus. Still in black clothes and wearing his mask. His standing dummy beside him.

Inside the bump was unused masking tape and a knife that he had bought that day from the local supermarket with the blue label beginning with t.

He had a body to deal with at base.

A dead blonde-haired woman in a red dress.

He planned to cut her up and dump her in a skip. There was one or two that he knew of dotted around the place. There was one in Hope Street as well as Bothwell Street. If he had to, he could find others.

First, he took the dress off. He found it fiddly and awkward and the dress got ripped as he removed it. Then he put the body in the bath before cutting the head off and the limbs off the torso.

Finally, he cut the torso in two or tried to. The spine got in the way of the knife, and it broke.

He swore under his breath. The f curse word. He swore repeatedly when he saw he had cut himself on the thumb with the knife.

His blood could catch him out he knew. He hadn't served time before now and he was dammed if he was serving time. He would rather die first.

He grabbed the red dress and covered his thumb with it hoping nobody heard him before running the tap to wash the body parts before bagging them up in thick black bags.

A few drops of blood got into the bags. He didn't notice it. He was too busy thinking of getting to the skip and back without being seen. He took his clown mask off. It was hot now. He needed a drink. He changed into a pink tracksuit and walked to the skip with the bags in tow.

Nobody saw anything odd. He was just some guy putting out the rubbish. His red hair worked with his pink tracksuit. It looked smart. Almost trendy.

He touched his bushy beard. He needed to shave. But tonight, he will drink with friends and tell them the lie that he was ditched by his latest girlfriend for a rich doctor.

It will get him the sympathy vote.

He will drink well tonight.

Eleventh of November two thousand and twenty three. Three am.

At the pub he got chatting to a young blonde-haired girl who was thirty five years old. She had blue eyes and was very fat.

Her name was Jennifer and she didn't work for the NHS. She was in training to be a school teacher and was very cruel to the kids she was in charge of. She hated the smart ones as they used to show her up.

She bullied them. She used to call them names. Useless was a term she used of them. If she was in a good mood of course.

If she was in a bad mood, she punished them harshly for tiny crimes by making them scrub the toilets with a toothbrush. Male, female and unisex ones. All cleaned by the same toothbrush.

Talking in class was just one of these tiny crimes. Bulling was allowed. If you were bullied by the other kids you were punished for standing out.

Then the teacher bullied you more. Not only that but the victim had to apologise to the bully for letting them bully him or her.

After the apology was given the victim was harassed even more and punished for being bullied. Needless to say, bulling was spreading in her school garnock academy like the black death in the Middle Ages. Just nobody owned up to being bullied that was all.

Not even the ones who were bullied constantly by everyone else admitted it. They were having to say sorry for being born.

Jennifer loved bulling them. They reminded her of an old victim of hers. Elizabeth Louisa Mullen. A young kid with Asperger's with a brother with autism. Her fiancée was normal apart from his left arm. Jennifer had loved calling her names and forcing her to eat cold chips off the floor at school.

Jennifer didn't know that Elizabeth was now a world-famous author who "people watched" in her spare time. That was how the press put it. The truth was Elizabeth noticed stuff more then other people. Maybe it was the Asperger's. Maybe it was a result of years of constant bulling. Elizabeth was great at spotting stuff. It was like she ran on instinct. Instinct that would have kept her ancestors alive in Africa millions of years ago.

Instinct that kept her alive and watching her back.

Jennifer never had to watch her back. She had lots of school friends and bullied helpless children mercilessly.

Jennifer swapped numbers with the man she had met. He also had been a bully at school. He wanted to meet up with her but wasn't sure if she was free.

She agreed to meet up with him in Glasgow on the twenty first of November two thousand and twenty three at half eleven on the dot.

Twenty first of November two thousand and twenty three. Ten am.

The bus station was busy. The body of the blonde woman in the red dress had been found that morning chopped up in the skip full of building materials.

Naturally the police were looking for a builder who knew the Glasgow area.

The young police officer saw the body and noticed a cross on her left breast on her chest.

She knew then that the slasher had struck again.

Tenth of November two thousand and twenty three. Four pm.

She sat there with her blue jeans on black shoes and green, red fleece filled hooded jacket on. Her bleached dark brown hair and pointy nose made her look like a drug user that was coming down from a high.

Her faded blue jeans had seen better days and she travelled with a young smallish dark haired boy dressed in black.

That boy was her son. He was called John Watt. He was the oldest.

John had three brothers and two sisters. He looked after them and they were worried about their mum. She drank alcohol like a fish breathes water. By which I mean she was a raging alcoholic who hated people and a mean cow when drunk.

Her name was Alice Pidgeon, and she was wanted for an attack on a helpless disabled girl who had autism. The attack had left the girl badly shaken but unhurt.

How had Alice's life come to this? Wanted by the police for a terrible thing. She didn’t know. She didn’t understand. She had been drunk. She didn’t remember a thing.

Her mother was looking after the children today. Alice had agreed to let her mother look after the children in return to treat her eldest son to build a bear. He was fifteen on the fifteenth and Alice knew she wouldn’t see him then.

She would be in the clinic then getting clean of the drink. As part of the rules, she would also be getting treated for her HIV. She had just got the results back. She had HIV.

God knows what that kid must have thought of her. She maybe have been drunk, but she sort of remembered punching someone for mentioning AIDS.

Now she wanted to thank that kid. If she could only remember what she looked like.

She only remembered stand eight was important. She didn't remember why.

She also didn't know why the kid in the pink jumper with the red hair that was thinning out was looking terrified of her. She hoped the boy with her made her seem less terrifying.

No such luck.

The red girl looked a shadow of her former self. She looked like she was on hyper alert. That's because she was.

All her faith and confidence was gone, quite possibly forever. No longer could she feel safe in Glasgow.

Alice had no clue that she was the cause of it. She only knew what the kid would tragically discover is that the police are not there to serve the public. They are there to fool the public into behaving. There is no incentive to behave as the police and courts are on the side of the criminals and not the law fearing folk. Criminals get away with murder and disabled folk get ignored.

In short, the police are just chain smoking, coffee drinking doughnut eating wankers that would only care if the crime in question was against a normal person and not disabled women. Alice knew disabled women were third class citizens at best. Alice felt untouchable.

She told John. “Nobody messes with your mummy.”

It was as she left the bus station and headed in the direction of the college to go to Buchanan galleries that Alice met a friendly man.

He looked normal. Just a normal red haired man dressed in black with a scar down one cheek. He had a knife on him.

He took her away from her son and cruelly killed and raped her.

And the police didn’t respond to her panicked 999 call even when it went silent.

So, the man raped her again then dumped her body in kelvingrove.

Ryan Woods took the phone call when Alice's body was found. He knew it meant the Slasher was alive.

For Alice, Damien and Ryan salvation is impossible.

Printed in Great Britain
by Amazon

36893632R00128